P9-DES-968

Whose dark or troubled mind will you step into next? Detective or assassin, victim or accomplice? Can you tell reality from delusion, truth from deception, when you're spinning in the whirl of a thriller or trapped in the grip of an unsolvable mystery? You can't trust your senses and you can't trust anyone: you're in the hands of the undisputed masters of crime fiction.

Writers of some of the greatest thrillers and mysteries on earth, who inspired those who followed. Writers whose talents range far and wide—a mathematics genius, a cultural icon, a master of enigma, a legendary dream team. Their books are found on shelves in houses throughout their home countries—from Asia to Europe, and everywhere in between. Timeless books that have been devoured, adored and handed down through the decades. Iconic books that have inspired films, and demand to be read and read again.

So step inside a dizzying world of criminal masterminds with **Pushkin Vertigo**. The only trouble you might have is leaving them behind.

SHE WHO WAS NO MORE

PUSHKIN VERTIGO

Pushkin Vertigo
71–75 Shelton Street
London, WC2H 9JQ

Original Text © by Éditions Denoël,
1952 (*Celle qui n'était plus*)

Translation by Geoffrey Sainsbury

First published by Pushkin Vertigo in 2015

0 0 1

ISBN 978 1 782270 81 2

All rights reserved. No part of this publication may be
reproduced, stored in a retrieval system or transmitted
in any form or by any means electronic, mechanical,
photocopying, recording or otherwise, without
prior permission in writing from Pushkin Press

Text designed and typeset by Tetragon, London
Printed and bound by
CPI Group (UK) Ltd, Croydon CR0 4YY

www.pushkinpress.com

SHE WHO WAS NO MORE

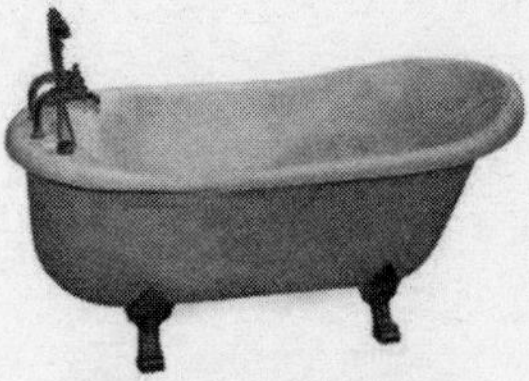

ONE

'Can't you keep still for a moment, Fernand?'

Ravinel halted in front of the window and drew the curtain to one side. The fog was getting thicker, forming yellow halos round the clusters of lights on the quay and green ones round the lamp posts along the roadway. Sometimes it thickened suddenly, drifting past in wreaths of smoke, at others it turned into a fine drizzle of glistening drops. Bits of the *Smoelen*'s forecastle, the portholes lit up, would come into view for a moment and then be blotted out. Now that Ravinel was standing still he could hear music from a record player. He could tell it was a record player because each piece lasted about three minutes, after which there was a pause while the record was changed. The sound came from the *Smoelen*.

'I wish it weren't there,' muttered Ravinel. 'Anyone on deck might see her coming. If they saw her enter the house…'

'Nonsense,' answered Lucienne. 'Mireille won't do anything to make herself conspicuous. Besides, it's a foreign ship. Why should foreigners take any notice of her?'

With his sleeve he wiped the window that had become misty with his breathing. Looking out over the railings of the tiny front garden, he could see to the left a stippled line of pale lights and strange constellations of red and green ones, the former like the candles flaming at the far end of a church, the latter phosphorescent as fireflies. It was quite easy for

Ravinel to follow the curve of the Quai de la Fosse, to pick out the semaphore on the old Gare de la Bourse, the light on the gate of the level crossing, the lantern that hung on the chains which at night closed the passage to the transporter bridge, and the anchor lights of the *Cantal* and the *Cassard*. On the right, another quay began, the Quai Ernest-Renaud. The street lamps were reflected by the wet pavements and railway lines. On board the *Smoelen* the phonograph was playing Viennese waltzes.

'She'll take a taxi,' said Lucienne. 'At any rate to the corner of the street.'

Ravinel dropped the curtain and turned round.

'No she won't,' he muttered. 'She doesn't throw money around like that.'

Another silence. Ravinel started pacing up and down the room again. Eleven steps between the window and the door. Lucienne was filing her nails. From time to time she held her hand towards the light which hung from the ceiling and turned it this way and that like some precious object. She had kept her coat on, though she had insisted on his changing into a dressing gown, taking off his collar and tie, and putting on his slippers.

'You see, you've just come in. You're tired and have changed into some comfortable clothes before sitting down to your supper… Got it?'

Oh yes, he understood all right. Only too well, with a sort of desperate clarity of mind. Lucienne thought of everything! And when he started to get the tablecloth out of the sideboard drawer, she pulled him up promptly in that husky voice of hers which was accustomed to giving orders.

'No. You don't want a tablecloth. You've just come in. You're all alone and can't be bothered to lay the table properly. You just picnic on the oilcloth.'

She had herself put a knife and fork for him. The slice of ham, still in its paper, she had thrown carelessly between the bottle of wine and the carafe of water. An orange stood on the box of Camembert.

'Quite a pretty picture!' he mused. 'A still life.' And he stood gazing at it for a while, frozen, unable to move, his hands sweating.

'There's something lacking all the same,' remarked Lucienne. 'Let's see… You change… You're going to have supper—all alone… You've no wireless to switch on… There! I have it! You glance through your day's orders. It's only natural.'

'But I assure you—'

'Hand me your dispatch case.'

On a corner of the table she spread out some typewritten sheets of paper at the head of which was printed a fishing rod and a landing net crossed like swords and the name of the firm he worked for: *Maison Blache et Lehuédé, 145, Boulevard de Magenta, Paris.*

It was then twenty past nine. Ravinel could have related minute by minute everything they had done since eight o'clock. First of all they had inspected the bathroom, making sure everything worked properly so that there was no chance of a hitch at the last moment. Fernand had wanted to fill the bathtub then and there, but Lucienne had objected.

'Use your brains. She'll want to look over the place and she'd wonder what the water was doing there.'

They nearly had an argument about it. Lucienne was in a

bad temper. Despite her outward coolness, you could see she was strung up and anxious.

'My poor Fernand! One might think you didn't know her. After five years!'

Which wasn't so far from the truth. Did he know her? He wasn't sure. It wasn't as easy as all that to know a woman. You sat opposite her at meals. You went to bed with her. You took her to the movies on Sundays. You saved up money to buy a little house on the outskirts of Paris. Good night, Fernand! Good night, Mireille! She had cool lips and tiny freckles at the base of her nose, but you only noticed them when you kissed her. Light as a feather when you picked her up. But, if she was thin, she was strong and wiry. A nice little thing. Insignificant, however. Why had he married her? Can anyone really answer a question like that? You're thirty-three. You've reached the marrying age. You're sick to death of hotels and cheap restaurants. It's no fun being a traveling salesman. When you're working out of Nantes all week, it's nice to go back at the weekend to that other little house at Enghien and find a smiling Mireille sewing at the kitchen table.

Eleven steps from the door to the window. A peep past the curtain. The three lit-up portholes in the *Smoelen*'s bow were lower now. The tide must be ebbing. A freight train from Chantenay trailed past, the wheels creaking, and one after another the roofs of the cars slid slowly under the semaphore in a mist of fine rain. An old German caboose brought up the rear with a red light hanging above the buffers. When it had passed, the *Smoelen*'s record player was audible once more.

At a quarter to nine they had each had a small brandy

to keep their courage up. It was after that that Ravinel had changed into his slippers and dressing gown. The latter had several holes burned in it by sparks from his pipe. Lucienne had arranged the things on the table. Silently. That was the trouble: they could find nothing to talk about. The train from Rennes had gone by at nine sixteen, sending beams of light sweeping across the ceiling. It seemed a long time before the rhythm hammered out by its wheels finally died away.

The train from Paris wasn't due till ten thirty-one. Another hour to wait! Lucienne went on silently filing her nails. The alarm clock on the mantelpiece ticked breathlessly. Occasionally something went wrong with the works. Its pulse would miss a beat, then right itself, though continuing on a slightly different note.

For a moment their eyes met. Ravinel took his hands out of his pockets and, clasping them behind his back, resumed his pacing, trying to obliterate the vision of this other Lucienne who was a stranger to him, a hard-featured woman with a scowl on her forehead. It was folly, what they were about to do, absolute folly… Unless…

Unless, for instance, Lucienne's letter had gone astray. Or Mireille might be ill, or…

He slumped down on a chair at Lucienne's side.

'I can't go on with it.'

'What's the matter? Afraid?'

He bristled at once.

'Afraid! No more than you are.'

'Then everything's all right.'

'It's only this waiting that gets me down. As a matter of fact I think I've got a temperature.'

11

She felt his pulse with her firm, expert hand. She made a face.

'You see! I'm getting something. And if I fall ill, that'll make a nice hash of things.'

She stood up, slowly buttoned her coat, then casually ran a comb through her dark curly bobbed hair.

'What are you doing?' stammered Ravinel.

'I'm going.'

'No. You mustn't.'

'Then pull yourself together. What is there to be afraid of?'

Were they to go over all that again? For the hundredth time? As if he didn't know Lucienne's arguments by heart! For days and days he'd turned them over, studying them one by one. He hadn't jumped at the idea—far from it!

His mind went back to Mireille. There she was, ironing in the kitchen, stopping now and again to stir something that was simmering in a saucepan. How well he had lied! Almost without effort.

'I ran into Gradère today. You must have heard me speak of him. No? Really? We did our military service together. He's doing insurance work now. Seems pretty prosperous.'

Mireille was ironing some underpants, the point of the iron going deftly round each button, leaving a smooth white trail from which rose a trace of steam.

'He kept at me for a long time, telling me I ought to take out some life insurance. At first I didn't take him very seriously. After all, you know what they're like. They're thinking of their rake-off, and you can't blame them. It's only natural… In the end, however, I had to admit there was something in it.'

She put the iron down on its stand and switched off the current.

'You see, in my line of business, there aren't any widow's pensions. And when you think of all the traveling I have to do… Accidents are only too easy. And if that happened, what would become of you? We've no savings to speak of.

'So in the end I let Gradère quote me rates. The premium isn't too stiff. Not when you consider the advantages. For if anything happened to me, you'd get a couple of million francs in cash.'

It sounded pretty good, that. A proof of his affection. Mireille was quite bowled over.

'Really, Fernand. You're so kind…'

But the hard part was still to come—to wheedle Mireille into taking out a similar policy for his benefit. That was a delicate subject. How was he to raise it?

He didn't have to. The wretched Mireille spared him the trouble.

'I've been thinking it over,' she said a week later, 'and I've come to the conclusion my life ought to be insured too. After all you never can tell who's going to live or who's going to die. And you'd be in a pretty pickle with no one to look after you.'

He had protested. Of course, he had to. But no more than was absolutely necessary, and in the end she had signed on the dotted line. That had been two years ago.

Two years. They'd had to wait that long. It was stipulated by the insurance company that if the insured person committed suicide within two years the contract was void. And you never knew what verdict might be brought in at an inquest. Lucienne, at any rate, was not the sort of person to take a risk like that. To go to so much trouble and then perhaps get nothing in the end!

Yes, it had all been carefully thought out, and a hundred other details too. In two years you can study a problem pretty thoroughly. No. There was nothing to be afraid of. Ten o'clock.

Ravinel got up from his chair and joined Lucienne who was standing at the window. The street was empty, glistening with wet. He slipped his hand under his mistress's arm.

'Don't take any notice. I can't help it… As soon as I start thinking…'

'Don't think.'

They stood side by side, motionless, the intense silence of the house weighing on their shoulders, behind them the alarm clock ticking feverishly. The portholes of the *Smoelen* were like pale full moons, growing still paler as the mist thickened. Even the phonograph seemed muffled by it. Ravinel hardly knew whether he was alive or dead. As a small boy it was like this that he had visualized the next world—a long wait in a fog. An interminable, terrifying wait. If he shut his eyes, it felt as though he were falling—a giddy, awful feeling, yet somehow pleasant at the same time. His mother would shake him.

'Whatever are you up to?'

'Nothing. Just a game.'

When he opened his eyes, he felt lost for a moment and vaguely guilty. Later on, when he was being prepared for his first communion the Abbé Jousseaume had questioned him.

'Any wicked thought? Any impure ones?'

And he had at once thought of this fog game. Obviously it was something forbidden. Impure, no doubt. Yet he had never altogether given it up. In fact he had even developed it to the point where he himself seemed to evaporate and become part of the fog. For instance, on the day of his father's funeral. It really had been foggy then, so thick that the hearse had looked like a sinking ship. And he had clearly had the feeling they were already in another world. It wasn't sad. Nor was it exactly gay. Just a supreme peace… On the other side of a forbidden frontier…

'Twenty past ten.'

'What?'

Ravinel started, finding himself once again in the poorly furnished, dimly lit room, standing beside a woman in a black coat who took a small medicine bottle from her pocket.

Lucienne! Mireille!

He took a deep breath. He was back on this side of the frontier now.

'Come on, Fernand. Rouse yourself. Here, give me the carafe.'

She spoke to him as though he were a boy. That's what he loved in her, in this Dr. Lucienne Mogard. Funny, wasn't it? She was his mistress. At moments it seemed quite incredible, almost monstrous.

Lucienne emptied the bottle into the carafe and gave the mixture a shake.

'Take a sniff. No smell whatever.'

Ravinel sniffed. She was right. The stuff was absolutely odorless.

'You're sure it's not too strong?'

Lucienne shrugged her shoulders.

'If she drank the lot, perhaps. Though even that's doubtful, and in any case she won't. She'll have a glass, two at the most. Trust me to know how it works. She'll fall asleep almost at once.'

'And—if there's a post-mortem—they won't find any trace?'

15

'My dear Fernand, as I've told you before, this isn't a poison. It's just a soporific and it's assimilated instantly. Now, you sit down at the table…'

'Already?'

They both looked at the clock. Twenty-five past ten. The Paris train was approaching Nantes. It should now be crossing the Bottereau yards and in five minutes it would be in the station. Mireille would walk quickly. It wouldn't take her more than twenty minutes. Somewhat less if she took the tram as far as the Place du Commerce.

Ravinel sat down and opened the paper containing the ham. The sight of the sickly pink meat almost made him vomit. Lucienne poured out some wine for him, then had a final look round. She seemed satisfied.

'I'll leave you now. It's time I went… Take it easy. Just be natural, and you'll see—it'll all come right.'

She put her hands on his shoulders and kissed him lightly on the forehead. At the door, she turned to have a last look at him. Doggedly he put a bit of ham in his mouth and started munching. He didn't hear Lucienne go out, but a certain quality of the silence told him he was alone and his qualms began gnawing at him more fiercely than ever. He did his best to behave as on any other day. He crumbled his bread, drummed a tune with the point of his knife on the table, glanced at a typewritten sheet on which were written:

10 'Luxor' reels	30,000	francs
20 pairs 'Sologne' boots	31,500	″
6 'Flexor' rods, heavy	22,300	″

But it was no good. He couldn't swallow another mouthful. A locomotive whistled in the distance, from somewhere in the direction of Chantenay, perhaps from the Pont de la Vendée. It was impossible to tell exactly, as the fog played funny tricks with sounds. Supposing he cleared out and threw the whole thing up… No. It was too late. Lucienne would have posted herself somewhere on the quay where she could keep an eye on the house. Nothing could save Mireille now. And all this for a mere two million francs! So that Lucienne could gratify her ambition and buy a practice at Antibes. Her plans were worked out to the last detail. She had as practical a mind as any businessman. Her brain was like a calculating machine, and a highly perfected one at that. Every project was neatly pigeonholed; mistakes were all but impossible. With her eyes half shut she would murmur:

'Wait a minute. We mustn't get this wrong.'

The right buttons would be pressed, wheels would start turning, and with a click out would come the answer, neat, precise, exhaustive.

With him it was just the other way round. He was always getting into a muddle over his accounts or forgetting which customer had ordered cartridges and which had asked him to quote a price for Japanese bamboos. As a matter of fact he was sick of his job. Whereas at Antibes…

He gazed at the shining carafe which magnified a piece of bread till it looked more like a sponge. Antibes… A smart shop—for he was to set up on his own too. In the window would be air guns for underwater shooting and all the gear for frogmen. Rich customers. And, with the sea in front and the sunshine, your mind would be full of pleasant, easy thoughts that didn't make you feel guilty. Banished the fogs of the north. Everything would be different. He himself would be a different man. Lucienne had promised he would. As though seeing the future in a crystal, Ravinel saw himself sauntering along the beach road in white flannels. His face was tanned. People turned to look at him.

The locomotive whistled again, almost under the window. Ravinel rubbed his eyes, went and pulled the curtain aside, and peered out. Yes that was the Paris-Quimper express all right. A five-minute stop at Nantes. Next stop Redon. And Mireille herself was sitting in one of those coaches whose windows threw long rectangles of light onto the wet road. There were empty compartments with lace antimacassars, mirrors, and pictures of beauty spots along the line. First class. And there were compartments full of picnicking sailors—third.

Glimpse after glimpse swept past, looking quite unreal and nothing whatever to do with Mireille. In the very last carriage a man was asleep with a newspaper over his face. When the caboose was out of sight, Ravinel suddenly noticed that they were no longer playing the phonograph in the *Smoelen*. The lights were out. No portholes visible now.

Mireille would be already getting out of the train. In a minute she would be walking alone, her high heels sounding in the empty streets. Perhaps she would have her revolver in her bag. He made a practice of leaving it with her when he went on one of his rounds. Not that it was any use, for she didn't know how to use it. In any case there'd be no occasion for her to do so.

Ravinel held the carafe up to the light. The water was absolutely clear. No sign of any deposit. He dipped his finger in and licked it. A slight taste, but much too slight for anybody to notice unless he was on the lookout…

Twenty to eleven.

He forced himself to swallow a few mouthfuls of ham. He didn't dare leave his chair now. It had been settled: Mireille was to surprise him sitting at the kitchen table, alone, tired, depressed.

And suddenly he heard those heels of hers on the pavement. He couldn't be mistaken. Not that she made a lot of noise. It was only just audible, yet he could have recognized her step from among a thousand others, a slightly jaunty step made staccato by the narrowness of her skirt. The gate hardly creaked at all. Then silence. Mireille walked up to the front door on tiptoe and turned the handle. Suddenly aware that he was forgetting to eat, Ravinel helped himself to some more ham. Try as he might, he couldn't sit squarely at the table. He was afraid of that door behind his back. Mireille was certainly on the other side of it by now, listening intently. Ravinel coughed, made a noise with the bottle as he poured out some more wine, and rustled the sheets of paper. Was she listening for the sound of kisses?

She threw open the door. He swung round.

'Mireille!'

Her coat was open, revealing a navy blue suit in which she looked as slim as a boy. Tucked under her arm was her bag, the big black one with her initials, M.R. With her thin hand she pulled up her gloves. She wasn't looking at her husband, but inspecting the room—the sideboard, the chairs, the closed window, the table, the orange standing on the box of Camembert, the carafe. Advancing a couple of steps, she lifted her little veil, in which raindrops had been caught as in a spider's web.

'Where is she? Tell me where she is.'

Ravinel got up slowly, looking puzzled.

'Who do you mean?'

'That woman—I know all about it… It's no use lying to me.'

Mechanically he pushed his chair under the table. With a slight stoop, his forehead puckered, his hands hanging open at his sides, he faced her. He heard himself laugh.

'My dear Mireille! What are you talking about? What on earth's come over you?'

At that she sank onto a chair, buried her head in her arm, and burst into sobs, her hair straggling over his plate of ham. Ravinel was taken aback. He couldn't help being touched, and he stood over her, patting her shoulder.

'Come on, Mireille. Calm yourself. Then you can tell me all about it… So you thought I was carrying on with another woman, did you? My poor child! You'd better see for yourself whether there's any sign of one. Yes, you must. I insist. You can explain things afterwards.'

He lifted her, holding her up, led her away, while she clung to him, weeping on his chest.

'We'll have a good look round. You needn't be afraid.'

He kicked open the bedroom door and switched on the light. He spoke loudly, with affectionate roughness.

'Look! Just the bed and the wardrobe. Nobody under the bed. Nobody in the wardrobe. And can you smell anything? Take a good sniff. Just a little stale tobacco smoke, because I always have a pipe before going to sleep. As for any scent, not a trace! Now for the bathroom. After that we'll do the kitchen. Oh yes, we will.'

He showed her everything, even opening the refrigerator.

Mireille dabbed her eyes and began to smile through her tears. He drew her back into the dining room.

'Well? Convinced? What a silly girl! Not that I mind your being jealous. It's rather sweet. But to come on a journey like this! And in November. Somebody must have been telling you some dreadful stories.'

He sat down, but instantly jumped up again.

'There! I'd forgotten the garage.'

'No, Fernand. You mustn't joke about it.'

'All right. Now tell me all about it. Here, take this chair. I'll switch on the heater. Tired?... But I don't need to ask. You look washed out. Now sit back and relax.'

He brought the heater close to her, relieved her of her hat, and sat down on the arm of her chair.

'An anonymous letter, I suppose?'

'If it had only been that. It was Lucienne who wrote.'

'Lucienne! Have you got the letter with you?'

'I should think I have.'

She opened her bag and produced an envelope. He snatched it out of her hand.

'Good heavens! That's her writing all right.'

'What's more she made no bones about signing it.'

He pretended to read the letter he knew by heart, the three pages which Lucienne had written the day before, sitting in front of him.

> *She's a little red-haired thing hardly out of her teens, a typist who works at the Crédit Lyonnais. She comes to see him every evening. I hesitated for a long time before making up my mind to write to you, but in the end…*

Ravinel was on his feet now, pacing up and down the room with his fist clenched.

'It's past all belief. Lucienne must have gone clean out of her head.'

He slipped the letter into his pocket, trying to make the action seem absent-minded. He looked at the clock.

'It's a bit late now to get hold of her. And in any case she'll be at the hospital as it's Wednesday. It's a pity. We'd get this business cleared up at once. But she'll have to answer for it, believe me.'

He stopped abruptly and opened his arms in a gesture of incomprehension.

'Someone who calls herself a friend… Someone whom we've looked upon almost as one of the family… To do a thing like that!'

He poured himself out a glass of wine and drank it at a gulp.

'Would you like something to eat? You mustn't let it put you off your food.'

'No, thanks.'

'Some wine, then?'

'No. Just a glass of water.'

'If you'd rather.'

He took the carafe with a firm hand, filled up a tumbler, and stood it by her.

'Unless someone's copied her handwriting…'

'Go on! I wouldn't be taken in for a moment. And look at the notepaper. And the postmark. Nantes. Posted yesterday. I got it at four o'clock this afternoon. You can imagine what a blow it was.'

She wiped her cheeks. She stretched her hand out towards the glass.

'I didn't hesitate a second, but made straight for the station.'

'That's you all over.'

Gently Ravinel stroked her hair.

'Perhaps the truth is that Lucienne's jealous,' he murmured. 'She can see we're very united. There are people like that— can't bear to see others happy... We may have known her a long time, but have we any idea what really goes on inside her?... Though I must say she looked after you wonderfully three years ago. There was nothing she wouldn't do. In fact, she really saved your life. You know, things looked pretty black at one moment. Still, that's her job admittedly. And of course you might have pulled through anyhow. People don't often die of typhoid these days...'

'Yes, but she was so kind. Thought of everything. And the way she had me taken all the way to Paris in an ambulance.'

'All the same, she might have been thinking even then of making mischief between us... For now I come to think of it, I suppose she did take a fancy to me. Sometimes I was surprised we met so often, but it never really struck me—not in that light... Do you think she can have fallen in love with me?'

For the first time Mireille's face lit up.

'What?' she exclaimed. 'An old duffer like you?'

She drank the water slowly and put the empty glass back on the table. Then, seeing Fernand had turned pale, she took his hand and added:

'Don't be cross. I was only teasing. It's my turn to take it out on somebody!'

23

TWO

'You didn't tell your brother about it, I hope.'

'Of course not. I hadn't time. Besides I'd have been too ashamed.'

'So nobody knows you've come here?'

'Nobody. It's nobody's business but mine.'

Ravinel lifted the carafe.

'A little more.'

In a leisurely way he filled the glass again and began gathering up his papers. *Maison Blache et Lehuédé.* For a moment he was pensive.

'I can't see any other explanation,' he said at last. 'Lucienne wants to come between us. Look back. It's just a year since she had that temporary job in Paris. Why shouldn't she have lived in the hospital? Or in a hotel? No, she had to come and live with us.'

'We were bound to invite her. After all she'd done for me…'

'I know. I don't deny it. But that doesn't alter the fact that she fastened on us like a leech. And if she'd stayed much longer she'd have been ruling the roost. You were beginning to obey her like a servant.'

'You can talk! I suppose she never sent you running errands!'

'I wasn't the one to cook special dishes for her.'

'But you typed out her letters all right.'

'A strange girl,' said Ravinel. 'Whatever could she hope for in sending you that letter. She must have guessed you'd come here post-haste. And she knew I'd be alone when you got here and she'd be found out at once.'

Mireille seemed disturbed and Ravinel experienced a little pleasure. That she should find excuses for Lucienne was something he couldn't allow.

'How could she do such a thing?' muttered Mireille. 'I'm sure she's good at heart.'

'Good! You obviously don't know her.'

'I know her as well as you do. You can't deny that.'

'Not a bit of it. I've seen her here on the job. You've no idea what she's like in her own world. With the nurses for instance… Treats them like dirt.'

'Go on!' She tried to get up, but fell back into the armchair. She ran her hand across her forehead.

'What's the matter?'

'Nothing. Just a little giddy.'

'If you fell ill here, that would put the lid on it. Anyhow it wouldn't be Lucienne who looked after you this time. I'd see to that.'

Mireille yawned and with a tired gesture brushed her hair back from her forehead.

'Help me up, will you? I'd better lie down for a bit. I'm so tired, I…'

He lifted her up and she lurched forward, grasping the corner of the table.

'My poor child. To get in a state like that…'

He dragged her into the bedroom, her legs giving beneath her and trailing behind. One shoe fell off. Ravinel was out of breath when he finally rolled her onto the bed. She was white as a sheet and seemed to have difficulty in breathing.

'I think—I made a mistake to...'

It was no more than a whisper, but there was still a flicker of life in her eyes.

'Weren't you to have seen Germain or Marthe one of these days?' he asked.

'Not till next week.'

He stretched her out and threw a blanket over her legs. Her eyes followed him all the time, and a sudden misgiving came into them as a thought tried laboriously to take shape in her mind. 'Fernand!'

'What?'

'That glass of...'

There was no longer any point in lying to her. He began to move away from the bed, still followed by those eyes, those imploring eyes.

'Go to sleep,' he said.

Her eyelids quivered, once, twice. There was now only the tiniest glint of life in her pupils. Then it too went out and her eyes slowly shut. Ravinel ran his hand roughly over his face like a man who has walked into a spider's web. Mireille was motionless now. Her reddened lips were parted showing a row of pearly teeth.

He left the room and groped his way across the hall. He felt a bit unsteady. On his retina was stamped the image of Mireille's eyes which, sometimes glowing, sometimes fading, seemed to follow him through the darkness.

In a few quick strides he was at the garden gate, which Mireille had left ajar.

'Lucienne!' he called softly.

She promptly emerged from a shadow.

'Come on,' he said. 'It's over.'

She led the way back into the house.

'See to the bath,' she ordered.

But, instead of doing so, he followed her into the bedroom, picked up the stray shoe and put it on the mantelpiece, which he had to clutch to steady himself. Lucienne lifted up Mireille's eyelids one after the other.

He could see the white eyeballs, on which the lusterless iris seemed to be painted. He wanted to look away, but he was too fascinated. He knew that every movement Lucienne made was being engraved on his memory like some gruesome tattooing.

He had once read a magazine article about the truth drug. Supposing the police were to…

He trembled, folded his hands, then, horrified by this gesture of supplication, put them quickly behind his back. Lucienne was trying to find Mireille's pulse. Her long nervous fingers felt their way like some nimble creature looking for the artery before biting. In a moment they were still. They had found the place. Without turning her head she said again:

'Go on. Get the bath ready.'

That was her doctor's voice, curt, authoritative, the voice that was so reassuring when he thought there was something the matter with his heart. Finally he dragged himself away, went into the bathroom and turned on the tap. The water gushed into the tub with such a frightening noise that he instinctively reduced the flow.

'What's the matter now?' called out Lucienne.

He didn't answer and she came to the door.

'The splash,' he muttered. 'It might wake her up.'

She didn't bother to answer. Defiantly, she went up to the tub and turned both taps full on. Then she went back to the bedroom. Steadily the level of the water rose, greenish bubbling water over which hovered a cloud of steam, which condensed in a fine mist on the upper part of the tub, on the walls, and on the glass shelf over the washbasin. On the mirror too, and in it Ravinel could now only see a misty, unrecognizable image of himself. He put his hand in the water as though testing the temperature, as if he really was getting a bath ready for someone.

When he stood up, his temples were throbbing. The truth had suddenly struck him. Yes, struck him. That was the right word. It came like a blow, like a punch in the face. He realized what he was doing and it made him tremble from head to foot.

Fortunately it didn't last. In a few seconds it was all quite different. It wasn't he, Ravinel, who was guilty. No one was. Mireille had drunk a soporific. A bathtub was filling up. That was all. There was nothing terrible about it, and nothing which had anything to do with crime.

Admittedly he had poured out a glass for Mireille. But he had poured many a glass before. It was an everyday matter and didn't feel any different this time. Mireille had drunk the stuff herself. She needn't have. And that made it more or less her own fault. Like an illness contracted through one's own folly. Poor Mireille. No one was responsible for the simple reason that no one hated her. No one could—she was too insignificant.

And yet, when he went back into the room… It was like

some ridiculous dream. Perhaps he really was dreaming. No, he wasn't. The water still poured into the bath—with a deeper sound now—and the body was still on the bed. The shoe, too, was still on the mantelpiece. Lucienne was calmly rummaging in Mireille's handbag.

'I say!' exclaimed Ravinel.

'I was just looking for her ticket. She may well have taken a return. We have to think of everything. What about my letter?'

'She gave it me. I've got it.'

'Where is it now?' she demanded.

'In my pocket.'

'Burn it. Straight away. You might forget. There, in that ashtray by the bed.'

Ravinel held the envelope up and lit the corner with his lighter. He didn't drop it until it began to burn his fingers. The blackened paper curled up on the ashtray.

'Did she tell anybody she was coming?'

'Nobody.'

'What about Germain?'

'No. I asked her specially.'

'Hand me that shoe.'

As he took it, he had to choke a sob in the back of his throat. Lucienne put it back on Mireille's foot.

'The tub,' she said. 'It must be full enough.'

Ravinel moved now like a sleepwalker. He turned off the taps and the sudden silence was abysmal. A distorted face was reflected back to him in the still rippling surface of the bath water. A bald head. Thick bushy eyebrows, slightly reddish. A little toothbrush mustache under a queer-shaped nose. An energetic face, almost brutal, which led people to think

30

he was quite different from what he was. He had even been taken in by it himself. Only Lucienne had seen through it at the first glance.

'Hurry up,' she said.

He started, and came back to her. Lucienne had pulled Mireille up into a sitting position and was trying to get off her coat. Mireille's head wobbled from side to side.

'Come and hold her.'

Ravinel clenched his teeth and did as he was told, while Lucienne proceeded deftly to remove the coat.

'Keep her upright.'

Ravinel held his wife against him as though embracing her. It was ghastly. It was a relief when he was allowed to lay her back on the pillow again. He wiped his hands, breathing heavily. Lucienne folded the coat up carefully and took it into the dining room, putting it down by Mireille's hat. Ravinel sat down. He had to.

It was done. It was no longer possible to say to himself:

'There's still time to change our minds.'

That thought had come to him several times. It had helped to hold him up. Perhaps... at the last moment... In fact, so long as it could be postponed it remained something merely imaginary. That was consoling. So long as it was merely imaginary it wasn't true...

It was true now.

Lucienne came. She touched his hand.

'I feel awful,' he said. 'I can't help it. I'm doing my best.'

'I'll take her shoulders,' she answered. 'You take the legs.'

He had to go through with it, or he'd never hold up his head again. Almost a matter of honor. He grasped Mireille's ankles. And, as he lifted her, absurd phrases kept running through his head.

'Don't worry, Mireille. You won't feel anything… You see, I can't help myself… I swear I never wanted to do you any harm… For that matter, I'm a sick man myself, and it won't be long before I'm carried off with a heart attack…'

He was on the brink of tears. With her heel, Lucienne kicked open the bathroom door. She was as strong as any man. Besides, she was used to dealing with bodies.

'Right. Lower her down. On the edge of the bath. You can leave the rest to me.'

Ravinel drew back so precipitately that he bumped into the glass shelf and nearly knocked over the tumbler. Lucienne let Mireille's legs slip into the water, then her whole body. Only a little water splashed onto the tiled floor.

'Now for the andirons. Quick. The ones in the dining room fireplace.'

Ravinel went off.

'It's over. It's over. She's dead…'

The words kept throbbing inside his skull. He could no longer walk straight, and, in the dining room, he stopped to drink a large glass of wine. A locomotive whistled under the window. The slow train from Rennes, no doubt… A little soot had fallen on the andirons. Should he clean them?… No. No one would ever know…

Carrying the andirons, he stopped in the bedroom, unable to take another step. Through the bathroom door he could see Lucienne stooping motionless over the bath. Her left arm was invisible, plunged in the water.

'Put them down.'

Ravinel could hardly recognize her voice. He dropped the andirons just inside the doorway and Lucienne stretched out with her free hand and took them. Upset as she undoubtedly was, she didn't make a single useless movement.

The andirons were to keep the body under the water. Ravinel lurched back into the bedroom and, burying his face in the pillow, gave vent to his pent-up feelings. Images kept coming up at him from the past: the first time he'd taken Mireille to see the little house at Enghien; the discussion as to where to put the wireless set; Mireille's delight at the new Renault he had bought. Then other vaguer images—a motorboat at Antibes, a garden full of flowers, a palm tree...

Lucienne had turned on the tap over the washbasin. Ravinel heard her put down the bottle of eau de cologne. She washed her hands and arms methodically as after an operation. She had been frightened all the same. Oh yes she had! Theories are all very well. It's easy enough to hold human life cheap and talk cynically about the end justifying the means. But when it comes to the point... Death was death, just the same, even an easy, painless one, and you couldn't laugh it off like that. No, he would never forget the look on Lucienne's face when she'd turned round to pick up the andirons. An agonized look. A reassuring one—for him. For it brought her down to his level. They were partners now, accomplices, and she could never leave him. In a few months they could be married. Still there was plenty of time to think of that. They hadn't yet worked out their plans for the future.

Ravinel wiped his eyes, surprised that he could have wept so much. He sat up on the edge of the bed.

'Lucienne.'

33

'Yes? What is it?'

She had recovered her normal everyday voice. He felt sure she was powdering her face and making up her mouth.

'Suppose we went right through with it this evening?'

Lucienne promptly appeared, her lipstick in her hand.

'Suppose we—took her away?' Ravinel went on.

'Have you lost your head? After working everything out to the last detail—'

'I'm longing to—to get it over.'

Lucienne gave a last glance at the bathtub, switched off the light, and gently shut the door.

'What about your alibi? You know very well the police may suspect you. Still more the insurance company. You've got to be seen, and by plenty of witnesses. Tonight, tomorrow, and the day after.'

'I know,' he said dejectedly.

'Come on, darling. Pull yourself together. The worst's over: you mustn't give way now.'

She stroked his cheek. Her fingers smelled of eau de cologne. He rose to his feet, leaning on her shoulder.

'You're right. So I shan't be seeing you till—till Friday.'

'I'm afraid not. I've got the hospital, you know. Besides, where could we meet? Not here!'

'I should think not!'

'And then—this isn't the moment for us to be seen about together. It might spoil everything, and it would be childish to take a risk like that.'

'The day after tomorrow, then. Eight o'clock?'

'Eight o'clock on the Quai de l'Île Gloriette. As we arranged. And let's hope it's a nasty night like this one.'

She went and fetched his things, his shoes, his tie, collar. Finally she helped him on with his overcoat.

'What'll you do with yourself during these two days, my poor Fernand?'

'I don't know.'

'You must have some customers to see in the neighborhood.'

'There are always customers to see.'

'Is your bag in the car? Sure you've packed everything? Razor? Toothbrush?'

'Yes. Everything.'

'All right. Let's go. You can drop me at the Place du Commerce.'

She carefully closed the doors, double-locking the front door, while he got the car out of the garage. The street lights seemed to be shining through layers of gauze. The fog was tepid, with a muddy smell. From the direction of the river came the sound of a diesel engine which kept misfiring. Lucienne got into the car beside Ravinel. He jerked the gears in, backed out, and stopped by the curb. Then he went back to the garage, shut the sliding door, fumbled irritably with the lock. He looked at the house, turning up his coat collar.

'We're off.'

The car moved forward slowly, pushing its way through the fog, which floated away on either side in straggling yellow trails and which stuck to the windshield, despite the efforts of the indefatigable wiper. A locomotive went by, disappearing almost at once, but leaving a track from which the fog had for a moment been swept and in which the rails glistened brightly.

In the Place du Commerce stood a row of lighted trolleys.

'You can drop me here. Nobody'll see me.'

She leaned over and kissed him on the temple.

'Now don't do anything silly. Keep your head. You know it had to be done.'

She slammed the door and disappeared into the fog. Ravinel was alone, his hands nervously clutching the steering wheel. He was convinced that this fog… It couldn't be an accident. It had a precise meaning.

There he was, he, Ravinel, sitting in a little metal box, and it was as though he were appearing before the Judgment Seat. He could see himself with his great bushy eyebrows. Fernand Ravinel. He wasn't really a bad chap at bottom. But there he was with his hands stretched out in front of him groping like a blind man. Through existence. Through eternity—through an eternal fog, at any rate. Nothing to be seen anywhere except a few shadowy figures. Deceptive figures. Mireille's, for instance.

Fog. There was no end to it. The sun would never shine again. He was convinced of that. He was in a land which had no frontier and which he'd never get out of. He was made of the same stuff himself. A wandering soul, a phantom. He had often been tormented by that idea—that he was nothing more than a phantom…

He let in the clutch and went round the Place du Commerce in bottom gear. Blurred figures were visible through the misty windows of the cafés. Lights. Lights everywhere. That's what Ravinel needed—light, and lots of it, enough to fill his carcass which seemed to hang loosely about him. He drew up at the Brasserie de la Fosse and went through the revolving door on the heels of a fair-haired girl who was laughing. Inside, he found himself in another fog, that of pipe and cigarette smoke, which lay in wisps between the faces and eddied round a tray of bottles which a waiter was carrying shoulder high.

The waiter was hailed on every side.

'What about that brandy I ordered?'

Coins clinked on the tables and on the cash desk, where a cash register worked incessantly. Someone ordered coffee for three.

'Three *filtres*?'

'Yes. Three.'

Balls rolled across the billiard table, colliding gently, just audible above the din. What a din! But Ravinel needed that too, for it was the sound of life. He found a seat in a corner, sat down and relaxed.

I've got here, he thought.

His hands rested on the table in front of him. Beside him was a square ashtray on each side of which was the word *Byrrh* in brown letters. Just an advertisement. Reassuring, though. A solid, comforting, everyday thing, pleasant to touch.

'Monsieur?' The waiter bent down with a mixture of deference and friendliness. Ravinel had a sudden idea.

'Some punch,' he answered. 'A large glass.'

'Very good, Monsieur.'

Little by little Ravinel forgot the night's work and the house on the quay. He was warm here. He smoked a cigarette. It smelt nice. The waiter was busy mixing his drink. His movements were careful, expert. A little more rum. Sugar. And the next moment the liquid was ablaze. A beautiful flame seemed to come spontaneously out of the air and hover over the punch. First it was blue, then orange. It was a delight to the eye. It reminded him of a calendar whose gorgeous colors he had admired as a little boy.

He drank, sip by sip, and the warm potent liquid went down his gullet like a river of gold. The sun rose again, banishing the shadows, the fears, the scruples, the horrors. After all he had a right to live a full, varied life, and he wasn't accountable to anyone. He felt as if he had at last shaken off something which for a long time had been suffocating him. For the first time, he was able to look straight into the eyes of that other Ravinel, the one that looked back at him from the mirror. Thirty-eight. His face, however, looked old already. Yet he hadn't really begun to live. Not really. Was it too late? Certainly not. Why should it be?

'Waiter! The same again. And bring me a timetable.'

Ravinel fished a postcard out of his pocket. Naturally it was Lucienne's idea that he should send a line to Mireille. *I'll be returning Saturday morning…* He shook his fountain pen. The waiter came back.

'By the way, what's the date?'

'The fourth…'

'Of course. How silly of me to forget. I've been writing it all day long. You wouldn't have a stamp, I suppose?'

The timetable was dirty and dog-eared, but Ravinel was beyond being disgusted by such things. He turned the pages over till he came to the Paris-Lyon-Méditerranée line.

Dijon, Lyon, the Rhône valley. The Riviera Express. His fingers moved down the list of stations. Antibes 7:44. This train went right up the coast to the Italian frontier and beyond. He turned over the pages. More trains to Italy. Through the Simplon or the Mont Cenis. He could almost see them as he gazed into his cigarette smoke—long trains with dark blue

38

sleeping cars and dining cars. He could see them rumbling with a leisurely rhythm through a clear, bright, starry night, a night in which there was no shame...

The punch left an aftertaste of caramel in his mouth. His mind was full of distant travel.

'We're closing now, Monsieur.'

It was now Ravinel's turn to throw some coins onto the table. He wouldn't take the change. With a lordly sweep of his arm he brushed aside the waiter, brushed aside the past, and dived at the revolving doors, which for a moment caught him in their arms and discharged him on the pavement. There he stopped for a moment, leaning against the wall. His thoughts were in a turmoil. For no reason at all a word came to his lips. Tipperary. Something the English have a song about. What on earth would it mean?

THREE

Only a day and a half to wait. Only a day. And now only a matter of hours. Ravinel had expected the wait to be terrible, but it hadn't been. Not in the least. Though, in a way, it had been worse—interminable and dreary. Time seemed to have lost its sense of proportion. Someone starting to do a five-year sentence might feel like that about time. And if it was a life sentence… But Ravinel banished the thought. Why should those words keep teasing him like an obstinate fly?

He drank a lot. Not to attract attention. Nor to get drunk. Simply to make the time pass a bit quicker. It's extraordinary how quickly an hour can slip away between two glasses of brandy. You don't have to think of anything particularly interesting—with the most commonplace details it's just the same. The hotel he'd stopped at last night, for instance. An awful bed. Still more awful the coffee in the morning. People coming and going all night long, and trains whistling. He ought to have left Nantes. Gone on a trip, to Redon for instance, or Anceny. He had been unable to leave, however. Each morning he had woken up in the wrong frame of mind. Everything seemed sharp and crystal clear—and utterly discouraging. Weighing his chances, they appeared so small that it simply wasn't worth while putting up a struggle. It wasn't till ten o'clock that confidence suddenly returned. A glow of light that made everything look different, the pros as well as the cons. By the time he barged into the Café Français, he was in a different mood altogether and could greet his friends breezily. There were always two or three of them there drinking coffee laced with rum.

'Hallo, Fernand!'

'I say! You're looking queer…'

So his looks betrayed something. Not much, though. It was easy to invent a reason. Toothache. A bad night.

'I had one last year,' said Tamisier. 'A molar. God! What pain!… I could have thrown myself out of the window.'

Ravinel listened gravely. Really, it was astonishingly easy to lie. You just said you had toothache, and the next minute you almost believed it yourself. With Mireille, for example, the other evening… Other evening indeed! Last night, to be exact! Impossible! It seemed ages ago.

No. It wasn't merely a question of time. It was more complicated than that. You'd suddenly become another man leading another life. Like an actor. With this difference, that when the curtain falls the actor is back where he was. Whereas…

'What's this new reel of yours like? The Rotor. Is there anything in it? I saw an ad for it in the *Pêche Illustrée*.'

'It's not bad. Not bad at all. Particularly for sea fishing.'

That was the *day after*. A November morning with wet pavements and a pallid sun trying to shine through the fog. From time to time a streetcar swept round the bend just outside the café, its wheels screeching against the rails. It wasn't an unpleasant sound, however—at least not to Ravinel's ear.

'All well at home?'

'Fine, thanks.'

Was that a lie? Not really. It all depended on who was speaking, the old man or the new.

'Not much of a life,' remarked Belloeil. 'Always on the road. Haven't you ever wanted to change to the Paris area?'

'No. In any case it's the territory of the most senior travellers. Besides, I get a much better turnover here.'

'For my part,' said Tamisier, 'I've never been able to make out how you came to choose a job like that. With your education.'

And he explained to Belloeil that Ravinel had taken a degree in law. But how could the latter explain something he'd never understood himself? Was it just that everything to do with water had an irresistible attraction for him?

'Still hurting?' asked Belloeil.

'A jab now and again.'

Water and poetry, yes. For there is poetry in instruments that are beautifully made, perfectly balanced and highly polished. A bit childish, no doubt. A sign that he'd never grown up. Perhaps he hadn't. But why should he want to? To turn into a Belloeil, selling shirts and ties and steadily pickling himself in alcohol? Slowly and patiently. Without hope.

So many people in the world! All anchored by invisible chains to their own particular hole and corner. Is there any point in telling them you despise them because you yourself belong to another race, because you're a nomad, because you sell airy playthings, lovingly displaying your fishhooks and flies on your customer's counter? It's a job, of course, like everyone else's. Only it's different. It has affinities with painting and literature. Difficult to explain. But there's no getting away from the fact that fishing is an escape.

An escape for what? That was the whole problem…

Ravinel started. Half past nine. For three quarters of an hour he had been turning over the events of the previous day.

43

'Waiter. A brandy.'

After that talk in the café, what had happened next? He had called on Le Flem, near the Pont de Pirmil. Le Flem had given him an order for three punt guns. They had been joined by a hairdresser who went fishing every Monday and never failed to come home with a huge pike. A lot of heavy fishermen's talk. The hairdresser didn't believe in artificial flies, and he wasn't won over until Ravinel had tied a Hitchcock then and there before his eyes, using bits of partridge feather for the wings. Ravinel had the knack. For tying flies, there was no one to touch him in France, possibly in the whole of Europe. It takes some doing, particularly if you haven't got a vise to hold the hook. The body and the hackle are comparatively easy, but tying on the wings—that really is tricky. It's certainly a knack, tying flies. An art, rather. For even when the fly doesn't imitate any known insect, the illusion is so perfect that it is difficult to believe it isn't real.

'My word!' said the hairdresser.

Brandishing an imaginary rod, Le Flem went through the motions of casting. Then his arms quivered as though he really had a fish at the end of his line.

'You see! That's the way to do it. Come here, little fellow…'

And he thrust an imaginary landing net under his victim. His movements were expressive. Ravinel could see at once that the hairdresser had fishing in his blood.

The hours had dragged on. In the afternoon he had gone to the moving pictures. Ditto in the evening. That night he had stayed at a different hotel. This time it was too quiet, and his mind had been obstinately haunted by Mireille. Not the Mireille in the bath. The one at Enghien, very much alive. It would have been nice if he could have talked things over with her.

'Look here, Mireille. What would you have done in my place?'

It was impossible to get away from the fact that he still loved her. Or rather that he was beginning to. Shyly. It was fantastic, monstrous if you like, and yet…

'Why! If it isn't Ravinell!'

Two men had stopped in front of him. One of them was Cadiou, the other a tall, spare man in a fur-lined jacket, who looked hard at him as though…

'Larmingeat,' said Cadiou, introducing his friend.

Larmingeat! That's who it was! Ravinel had known him as a schoolboy in a black smock who had helped him with his sums. For a second they stared at each other, then Larmingeat held out his hand.

'Fernand. Fancy meeting you again! It must be quite twenty-five years since we last saw each other.'

Cadiou clapped his hands.

'Three brandies.'

There was a moment of embarrassment all the same. To think that this was Larmingeat! This tall fellow with a beaky nose and cold eyes!

'What are you doing now?' asked Ravinel.

'I'm an architect. And you?'

'Oh, just a salesman.'

That was slightly embarrassing too. It established a certain distance between them. Larmingeat turned quickly to Cadiou.

'Yes. We were at school together. In Brest. And if I remember rightly we graduated at the same time. But what a long time ago!'

He warmed his brandy in the hollow of his hand.

'What about your parents?' he asked, turning back to Ravinel.

'They are both dead.'

Larmingeat sighed.

'His father was a master at the Lycée,' he explained to Cadiou. 'I can see him still, with his briefcase and his umbrella. He rarely smiled.'

That was quite true. He hardly ever smiled. For one thing, he had T.B. But there was no need for Larmingeat to know that. In fact Ravinel had much rather they talked of something else than his father, a dull stick of a man, always in black. It was really because of him that Ravinel had become fed up with his studies. Always saying: 'When I'm no longer with you,' and enjoining his son to work harder and harder. Sometimes at meals he would stop eating and contemplate him from under his enormous Ravinel eyebrows. Then a volley of questions would be fired at him. What was the date of the Treaty of Campo Formio, the formula for butane gas, the sequence of tenses in Latin. A precise, meticulous man, in whose brain all information was neatly classified. For him geography consisted of lists. Towns, mountains, rivers. History was a list of dates. Man himself was a list of bones, muscles, and organs.

When Ravinel took his examinations—that was the worst of all. To think of it was enough to make him break out into a cold sweat. And even now strange words would suddenly jump up at him out of the past, menacing as in a nightmare. Words like cretaceous or monocotyledonous. It's not with impunity that you're the son of a schoolmaster—at any rate of one like that.

What would Larmingeat say if Ravinel told him he had actually prayed for his father's death? He had. And he had watched intently for every sign of the approaching end. He had known enough about the symptoms. He knew the meaning of a little froth at the corner of the mouth, or that peculiar hollow cough in the evenings. And all his life he had known what it meant to be the son of an invalid. Always thinking of one's own health, conscious of one's temperature and of the least change in the weather.

'We don't live long in our family.'

That's what his mother used to say. And she backed it up by dying a few months after her husband, just fading away, worn out by years of worry and scraping.

He was an only child, Ravinel, and, though he was well in his teens when his parents died, it seemed to him ever after that he had always been an orphan. And he had remained rather like one. Something in him seemed to have been nipped in the bud. He always started if a door slammed or his name was called out and became nervous if a question was fired at him suddenly. Of course nobody asked him the date of the Treaty of Campo Formio nowadays. But that didn't make any difference: he was afraid of being caught on the wrong foot. Another thing: he was apt to forget his own telephone number or the number of his car. One day, perhaps, he'd forget his own name! An awful thought! He'd no longer be a son or a husband or anything else. Just a man among millions of others…

As a matter of fact, on second thoughts, it might be rather nice. Only, it would be one of those *forbidden* pleasures.

'Do you remember those outings to the Pointe des Espagnols?'

47

That was Larmingeat. Ravinel came slowly up to the surface.

'I'd like to have known Ravinel in those days,' said Cadiou. 'What they call a tough guy, I bet.'

'A tough guy?'

Larmingeat and Ravinel exchanged glances. They smiled at one another, and it was like sealing a pact. Because Cadiou couldn't possibly understand.

'Tough enough. In his way,' answered Larmingeat. Then he asked:

'Married?'

Ravinel caught sight of his wedding ring. He blushed.

'Yes. We live near Paris. At Enghien.'

'I know the place.'

There were pauses in the conversation. They had plenty of time to study each other. Larmingeat too wore a wedding ring. Occasionally he wiped his eyes, for he wasn't in the habit of drinking spirits. There were any number of questions Ravinel might have asked him. But what was the use? Other people's lives had never interested him.

'How's the housing programme getting on?' asked Cadiou.

'Not too badly.'

'What does it cost nowadays to build a bungalow? A decent one, but nothing out of the way.'

'It depends. Four rooms and a bathroom—a really well-fitted bathroom, mind you—it'd run you into a couple of million francs, I dare say.'

Ravinel called the waiter.

'Shall we make it the same again?' suggested Cadiou.

'Afraid I can't stop,' said Ravinel. 'Got an appointment. You'll excuse me, won't you, Larmingeat.'

They shook hands with him limply. Larmingeat looked a trifle put out, but he was too discreet to ask any questions.

'You might just as well stop and have lunch with us,' grumbled Cadiou.

'Another time.'

'That's a deal. And I'll take you to see the bit of land I've bought at the Pont de Cens.'

Ravinel hurried away. He had behaved awkwardly and he cursed himself for having lost his nerve. But he had always been sensitive. Was that his fault? Besides, under the circumstances… Would anyone else in his place?…

The hours dragged on. Darkness fell. In the evening he drove to a garage. Oil and grease. Gas. To be on the safe side, he had two cans filled up as well. That done, he drove slowly to the Place du Commerce, past the Bourse, and crossed the esplanade of the Île Gloriette. On his left was the port, the lights trembling on the broken surface of the Loire. A Liberty ship was moving downstream. He had never felt so close to things, so detached from himself. All the same his nerves were stretched taut and his chest contracted at the thought of the ordeal that lay ahead.

An interminable freight train rumbled past. Ravinel counted the cars. Thirty-one. Lucienne must have left the hospital by now. He would leave it to her to finish the work. After all, it was her idea, the whole thing… The canvas. He suddenly thought of the canvas. He knew very well it was in the back of the car, yet he couldn't keep turning round to make sure. A 'California' canvas sheet which he carried round as a sample, for he dealt in all kinds of camping equipment too. When he turned back, there was Lucienne, coming up noiselessly on her crêpe soles.

'Hallo, Fernand! All right? Not too tired?'

Before even opening the door, she took off a glove to feel his hand. Having done so, she made a face.

'You seem pretty jumpy to me. And your breath smells of drink.'

'I had to. I had to be seen by plenty of people—you said so yourself.'

He started up the car and they went along the Quai de la Fosse. It was the rush hour. Dozens of little white lights zig-zagged about, crossing each other and recrossing. Cyclists. Ravinel had to keep a sharp lookout. If he knew next to nothing about the inside of a car, that didn't alter the fact that he was an excellent driver. For a while he had to drive very cautiously, but after the transporter bridge the traffic thinned out and it was quite easy going.

'Give me the keys,' said Lucienne.

He backed the car into the garage and she shut the door. He would have liked a stiff brandy.

'The canvas,' said Lucienne.

She went up two steps and in through the door between the garage and the house. Ravinel pulled the canvas sheet out, then rolled it up. Suddenly he heard the sound he dreaded. A gurgling sound—the bathwater being run away. The waste pipe passed through the garage.

Driving along beside rivers, he had more than once seen a body fished out. An ugly sight, a drowned person. Black and swollen. A prod with a boathook goes right into the flesh.

The gurgling went on. He in turn entered the house. In the doorway of the bedroom, he stopped. The bathroom door was open and through it he could see Lucienne bending over. A final gurgle in the waste pipe. What was she looking at? She seemed to be examining something. The canvas fell on the floor. It had slipped from under his arm. Or perhaps he had simply dropped it. He really didn't know. He turned on his heel and went into the dining room. The bottle of wine was still standing there beside the carafe. He drank direct from the bottle. Gulp after gulp, until he was out of breath.

That was better! Now for it! He'd have to face it sooner or later. He retraced his steps and picked up the canvas sheet.

'Spread it out flat.'

'What?'

'The canvas, of course.'

Her face was hard, implacably hard. He had never seen it like that before. Going into the bathroom he spread the green canvas out on the floor, which was not big enough for it.

'Well?' he whispered.

Lucienne had taken off her coat and rolled up her sleeves.

'What can you expect? After forty-eight hours…'

The strange power of words! Ravinel suddenly felt cold. He felt cold for Mireille. But he felt he had to see, and he glanced into the bath.

A wet skirt clinging to the legs. The arms bent, the hands pressed to the neck…

He drew back sharply uttering a cry. He had caught a glimpse of Mireille's face, her hair, darkened by the water, plastered across her forehead and her eyes, looking like sea-weed. He had seen her teeth, her gaping mouth.

'Help me,' said Lucienne.

He leaned over the washbasin, feeling sick.

'Wait—a moment…'

It was ghastly. Though he had to admit that it was less so than he imagined. The bodies he had seen fished out of the water had been much worse. They must have been immersed much longer, a week perhaps.

He straightened himself, removed his overcoat, then his jacket.

'You take the legs.'

It was Lucienne who gave the orders. It was difficult to lift, bending down over the tub. Mireille's legs were stiff and icy cold. Water splashed down noisily as the body was dragged over the edge of the bath and lowered onto the canvas sheet. Lucienne promptly covered it, rolled it up. It was rather like doing up a parcel. Soon there was nothing visible but a cylinder of green canvas from which oozed a little water. The two ends were twisted to give them something to hold on to, and like that they carried the body down to the garage.

'You ought to have left the car door open,' said Lucienne.

They managed to haul the bundle in and stow it diagonally in the back of the car, from which the rear seat had been removed. For that matter it always was, to make room for all the gear he had to carry round.

'It would have been better to have tied her up with string.'

Like a parcel!

He regretted the remark at once. The words were those of a traveling salesman, not a husband.

'It's all right as it is, and we haven't any time to waste.'

Ravinel got out of the car and straightened himself. There! Another hurdle had been taken. It hadn't used up all his nervous energy, which expended itself in tics and jerks. He rubbed his head, blew his nose, scratched himself and clenched and unclenched his fists.

'Wait here for me. I'm going back to tidy up.'

'Not on your life!'

Nothing would have induced him to wait all by himself in that dimly lit garage. So they went back into the house together. Lucienne cleared the dining-room table, emptied the carafe, and rinsed it thoroughly. She mopped up the water on the bathroom floor. Then she put her things on. Meanwhile he had tidied up the bed and put back the counterpane, after which, finding nothing else to do, he had brushed his jacket. At last, when all was in order, they had a final look round, Ravinel in his overcoat, hat in hand, Lucienne carrying Mireille's bag, coat and hat. Satisfied, she turned toward him.

'Well?... Pleased?... Give me a kiss then.'

Heavens, no! Not there! Really that was a heartless thing to suggest. There were moments like that when he couldn't make her out at all, she seemed so utterly inhuman. He pushed her out into the hall, shut and locked the door. Then back to the garage. Before getting into the car he glanced at each of the tires. He drove out, then came back to shut the garage door. A moment's panic seized him at the thought that any casual passer-by might look into the car.

A minute later they were driving towards the station, choosing the less well-lit streets. In the Rue du Général Buat they jolted over the cobblestones.

'No need to drive so fast,' commented Lucienne.

But Ravinel was in a tearing hurry to leave the town and get out into the dark countryside. Gas pumps, red, white, flashed by, workmen's cottages, the walls of a factory. At the far end of an avenue the barriers of a grade crossing were lowered, their reflectors scintillating. It was now that fear surged up within him. He stopped behind a truck and switched off his lights.

'Keep your lights on, silly!'

Was she made of wood, this woman? The train passed. A freight train. Cars full of ballast, drawn by an old locomotive from whose cab a segment of light glared up into the sky. The truck moved forward. The way was clear. Ravinel would have said a prayer if he had been able to remember one.

FOUR

Ravinel was used to driving at night. He preferred it, for he liked being alone and liked it all the more when tearing through the darkness at top speed. At night there was no need to slow down even at a village. The headlights lit up the road fantastically, making it seem like a canal stirred by a slight swell. Sometimes he could almost imagine he was in a speedboat. Then suddenly it would be like shooting down the slope of a switchback: the white posts bordering the road at the turnings would sweep giddily past, their reflectors glittering like precious stones. It was as if you yourself were conjuring up with a touch of your magic wand this unearthly fairy world, round which was a dim, shadowy void with no horizon. You dream. You leave your earthly flesh behind, to become an astral body gliding through a sleeping universe. Fields, streets, churches, stations. Created on the moment out of nothing and then swept away into nothingness again. A touch of the accelerator is sufficient to destroy them. Perhaps they have never really existed. Mere figments, created by you and lasting no longer than your whim, except, now and again, for an image that stamps itself on your retina like a dead leaf caught on your radiator—yet even that is no more real than the rest.

Yes. Ravinel loved the night. They had already passed Angers, which was now no more than a cluster of lights behind them. The roads were deserted. Lucienne sat silent beside him, her hands tucked into her sleeves, her chin buried in her turned-up collar.

As a matter of fact, Ravinel had not driven particularly fast since leaving Nantes. He took the bends gently, as though taking pity on the inert body behind, which might be thrown from side to side. Indeed, he probably wasn't averaging much more than fifty kilometers an hour. At that rate they would still reach Enghien before dawn, as arranged. That is, if all went well. The engine had stalled once as they passed through Angers. Perhaps he ought to have had the carburetor cleaned. Silly not to have thought of it. A breakdown during this drive would be no joke. About as little as an engine failure in a flight across the Atlantic! Ravinel listened to the engine. It sounded all right, but he'd better keep it under observation.

He shut his eyes for a second. There are thoughts which bring bad luck. The airplane flying the Atlantic—he'd no business to think of a thing like that... A red light. He was overtaking a huge truck that spat out a thick cloud of fumes. The driver didn't leave him much room to pass, but Ravinel took a chance and accelerated. When he drew out in front of the truck, he suddenly realized he was right in the glare of the other's headlights. From his cab, the driver might be able to see into the car. Ravinel put his foot down hard, but the car didn't leap forward as it should have done. A bit of dirt in the feed line? It certainly seemed like it.

Lucienne was quite unconscious of it all. She was dozing. In any case she never did react to the things that worried him. Strange how little feminine she was. Even when they made love... How had she ever become his mistress? Which of them had really chosen the other? At first she had taken no notice

56

of him, behaved almost as if he wasn't there. She had seemed only interested in Mireille and she had treated her more like a friend than a patient. They were the same age, those two.

Had she sensed that their marriage stood on shaky foundations? Had she suddenly fallen for him? What had she found in him? He knew he wasn't much to look at. Nor was he amusing. As a lover, he was no more than mediocre.

On his side, he would never have dared touch her. She belonged to another world, refined, distinguished, cultured, the world which his father, the little black-coated provincial schoolmaster, had eyed from afar, with the respect of the poor. At first Ravinel had thought it no more than a woman's caprice. A strange caprice. Brief, hasty intercourse, sometimes on a consultation room couch, within a yard of an enameled trolley on which stainless-steel instruments were laid out under a sheet of gauze. Sometimes she would take his blood pressure afterwards, as she was anxious about his heart. Anxious? No. Even that wasn't certain by any means. For if at times she treated him as though she really minded, at others she dismissed his complaints quite casually, just brushing them aside with a smile. That was what was so maddening. She had him completely foxed. The most probable thing was…

The most probable thing was that she'd had her eyes wide open right from the start. She had needed an accomplice, or rather a tool, perhaps, and had cast her net the moment she saw him. Love… That didn't count. At least not what people ordinarily mean by the word. What had brought them together was not mutual attraction, but something residing in the deeper and darker recesses of the spirit. Was money the one thing that really mattered to her? No, it wasn't money, not for its own sake, at all events. It was the power that went with it, the prestige, the right to command. She had to reign: it was an imperious necessity. And of course he had come under her sway at once.

But that wasn't all. There was also in Lucienne a sort of anxiety. Something so slight, so fugitive, that you could never put your finger on it. All the same, you knew it was there. The sense of insecurity that belongs to people who aren't quite normal. Perhaps that's what had drawn them together, for he wasn't quite normal either, not normal in the sense others were—Larmingeat for instance. He lived like other men, he rubbed shoulders with other men, he even passed for a first-class traveler, but that was only an illusion…

He was going up a steep hill, and the engine wouldn't pull. No life in it at all. Certainly there was something wrong…

What was he saying? Oh, yes—that he lived a bit to one side of things. Like an exile. He didn't really belong. And she suffered from the same thing. Sometimes he even got the impression she was clinging to him, as though terrified. Was it possible they could ever live together? Did he really want it?

He jammed on the brake, blinded by someone's headlights. A car streaked by in a gust of air. Then the road was clear again, a yellow line running down the middle of it, the shoulders flanked by trees painted white head-high. Sometimes a falling leaf would look like a distant stone or hole in the road. Ravinel's thoughts were going round and round in a circle. He had a cramp in his left foot and was longing for a cigarette.

Lucienne crossed her legs, then carefully drew her coat over her knee. Ravinel had to make an effort to realize he had a dead body in the back of the car.

'It would have been shorter by Tours.'

Lucienne spoke without turning her head. He too looked straight ahead as he snapped back:

'The road's torn up between Angers and Tours. Besides, what difference does it make?'

If she wanted an argument about it, she could have one! He was quite ready. She said nothing, however, merely pulling a map out of the glove compartment and studying it by the light from the dashboard. That irritated him too. Maps were a man's province. Would he ever have thought of rummaging in her desk? As a matter of fact, he had never been to her flat. Somehow the opportunity seemed never to have presented itself. For that matter, they both led busy lives. In the daytime they might snatch an hour together at lunch, or he might call at the hospital and see her for a few minutes on the pretext of a consultation. Otherwise, it was she who came to the little house on the quay. It was there that they had worked out their plans.

What did he really know about Lucienne? What did he know of her past? She didn't open up easily. Once she had mentioned that her father had been a judge at Aix-en-Provence and that he had died during the war, unable to stand the hardships. Of her mother she had never spoken and, when he had tried to probe her the response had always been the same—a frown. Presumably she was still alive, but he was pretty certain Lucienne never saw her. Some family row, no doubt. At all events she never went back to Aix. Yet she obviously had some feeling for the South, since it was at Antibes that she wished to set up practice. No brothers or sisters. In her surgery there was a little photograph—at least there had been, but it had disappeared some time ago—the photograph of a very beautiful girl with fair hair and Scandinavian features.

Later on he would inquire about her. After their marriage. How funny that sounded! Unreal. He simply couldn't picture Lucienne and himself as a married couple. Come to think of it, they were both bachelor types. That was a queer thing to say, and he really couldn't explain it. It was true all the same. They looked it. They both had the little fads and fancies that belong to a bachelor existence. And while he was extremely attached to his own, he hated hers. To start with, the perfume she used—some flower or other—which mingled badly with the animal smell of her skin. Her signet ring, which she fiddled with incessantly as she talked. It might have looked all right on a banker's finger or a big industrialist's. But on hers... Then there was the way she wolfed her food, and her always wanting her meat almost raw. Occasionally there was a touch of vulgarity in her movements or her speech. It didn't often show through—she was too well brought up for that—but now and again she would come out with a coarse laugh or look at you with the effrontery of a fishwife. Even physically, there were things he found hard to put up with—her thick wrists and ankles, her flat chest. And when she was alone she smoked thin black cigarettes, a habit she'd picked up in Spain. And how they stank! By the way, what had she been doing in Spain, anyway? There was one thing you could say for Mireille: no mystery in her past...

After La Flèche the country became more hilly. Sheets of mist lay in some of the hollows depositing fine droplets on the windshield. He had to take some of the hills in second. What filthy stuff it was, the mixture they sold nowadays as gas. No guts in it whatever, and it played hell with your engine.

Half past ten...

Not a soul stirring. They could have got out of the car and dug a grave by the side of the road—nobody would have stopped them... A dog in a ditch... No. He shouldn't say a thing like that. It wasn't fair to Mireille. She deserved better. With a sad tenderness he conjured up a picture of her. What a pity they hadn't been of the same race. A little house-wife so sure of herself, who loved frills and flounces, adored Technicolor films, and put cacti everywhere in tiny little pots. She thought herself superior to him, criticized his choice of ties and made fun of his baldness. She had never been able to make out why, on some days, he wandered gloomily about the house with a scowl on his face, his hands thrust deep into his trouser pockets.

'What on earth's the matter with you, my precious?... Do you want to go to the movies?... If you're bored here, you've only to say so.'

No he wasn't bored. It was something much worse than that. He was *sick to death*—that was the only way to put it. Sick of life, sick of everything. What's more, he always would be. He knew that now. It was something fundamental, irremediable. Now that Mireille was dead, was anything changed?

Perhaps... Perhaps later on, when they had settled down to a new life at Antibes...

A vast plain stretched out on each side of the road. It made it seem as though the car were not advancing at all. With her gloved hand, Lucienne cleaned a patch of the window and gazed out at the monotonous landscape. Right in front, on the horizon, were the lights of Le Mans.

'Cold?' he asked.

'No.'

On the sexual side, things hadn't gone any better with Mireille than with Lucienne. Possibly it was his own fault. Lack of experience. Or it had been his luck to come upon nothing but frigid women. Mireille had done her best to pretend, but he had never been taken in. She had remained completely unmoved, even when she had clutched at him with an ardor that was meant to be ecstatic. As for Lucienne, she had never bothered to pretend. Love-making left her cold, icy cold, if it didn't positively irritate her. That was the difference between them. Mireille took her duties seriously, and it was a wife's duty to respond in the flesh. Strange that she shouldn't succeed. She was so feminine, so human, that there ought to have been a streak of sensuality in her somewhere.

For his part, he could no longer take anything seriously. Or rather, what he could have taken seriously had no name: it was without form and void. Lucienne knew. He could tell that by the way she looked at him sometimes. And Mireille...

Ravinel pulled himself up. After all he had killed Mireille. Or hadn't he? That was just the point—he couldn't bring himself to believe he had committed a crime. Crime had always seemed to him something monstrous. And it still did! To be a real criminal you had to be a savage, bloodthirsty brute. And he wasn't in the least. He'd have been quite incapable of sticking a knife into anybody or even pressing a trigger. At Enghien there was a loaded revolver in his desk. It was the managing director, Davril, who had advised him to get one. When one's constantly on the road, particularly at night... But at the end of a month he had slipped it into a drawer, where it had made grease spots on his papers. For he'd have been no more capable of using it than Mireille. Even less perhaps. As for shooting at her...

No, his crime, if it was one, was negative, consisting of a whole chain of despicablenesses which he'd allowed himself to slide into through indifference. If a judge—a chap like Lucienne's father—were to ask him what he'd done, he could in all good faith answer: nothing. And since he'd done nothing he regretted nothing. Repentance—that came to much the same thing. What was he to repent? Unless it was being made as he was, and that was meaningless. You can't help the way you're made.

A signpost. Le Mans 1½ kilometers. Some big white buildings. Garages. Then the road passed under a steel bridge, after which it was flanked by low houses.

'You'll avoid the center, I suppose.'

'No. That's the shortest way.'

It was nearly half past eleven, and people were pouring out of the movies. Wet pavements. Here and there a café still lit up. On the left, two policemen, wheeling their bicycles, were crossing a square. Then another suburb, whose streets were lit by gas. More low houses. Garages. Gas pumps. Leaving the cobblestones, they were once more out on the blacktop road. Another railway bridge, with a locomotive, shunting. A moving van passed, going in the opposite direction. Ravinel accelerated to seventy-five. In a few minutes they'd be in the Beauce. An easy road as far as Nogent-le-Rotrou.

'There's a car overtaking you,' said Lucienne.

'Yes. I've seen it.'

The glare of its headlights seemed to fill the car with a golden dust, so thick that you were tempted to brush it aside with your hand. The car passed, cutting in too soon. A Peugeot. Half blinded, Ravinel swore. In no time the Peugeot had shot ahead growing visibly smaller every second. Then it rose up on the horizon, thrusting its two tusks of light into the sky. Couldn't have been doing a kilometer less than a hundred and ten an hour. It was just at that moment that the engine spluttered, then faded out. Ravinel tried the starter, but it was no good. The car was still rolling and instinctively he drew across to the side of the road, put on the brake and switched off his headlights.

'What on earth are you doing?' Lucienne asked aggressively.

'Can't you see? The engine's conked out. Probably the carburetor.'

'Clever of you!'

As though he'd done it on purpose. And so close to Le Mans. At a place where there was quite a bit of traffic about even at this time of night. He got out of the car with a tight feeling in his chest. A sharp little breeze drifted through the leafless trees. Every sound carried with extraordinary distinctness. He could hear the buffers telescoping as the locomotive bumped into a line of trains, then its puffing as it slowly towed them away. A driver was hooting at every bend in the road. As he lifted the hood, Ravinel had the sensation of being hemmed in by people on every side.

'Bring me the flashlight.'

She brought it, peered under the hood at the hot engine smelling of oil and gasoline.

'You'd better be quick.'

But Ravinel had no need of advice. He got to work at once. He had to dismantle the carburetor—he felt sure that was where the trouble was. The important thing was not to lose the screws. They were small enough! And his and Lucienne's whole future depended on them. Just one of those tiny bits of metal lost, and… Sweat broke out on his forehead and his eyes smarted. Sitting on the running board, he carefully laid the parts of the carburetor out in front of him. Lucienne paced up and down in the middle of the road.

'You'd do better to help me.'

'Perhaps I had. It might go a bit quicker. To think that—'

'To think what?'

'Don't you realize that the first motorist who passes may ask what the trouble is?'

'And if he does?' He picked up the feed line.

'He might want to lend a hand, and then…'

He was busy blowing through the feed line to clear it. He blew so hard it made his temples throb, and that was all he could hear. When he stopped she was still speaking and he just caught the words:

'…the police.'

What the devil was she driveling about? Ravinel wiped his eyes and looked at her. She was afraid. Not the slightest doubt about it—she was scared stiff. She got her bag out of the car. He sprang to his feet and, with the feed line still between his lips, he mumbled:

'Look here! You're not going to clear out?'

'Listen, you fool!'

A car. Coming from Le Mans. It was on them before they knew where they were. In the glare of its headlights they felt absolutely naked.

'In trouble?' asked a cheery voice. 'Anything serious?'

They could just make out the outline of a large truck. The driver was leaning out of the cab, the glow of his cigarette plainly visible.

'No,' answered Ravinel. 'It's all right now, thanks.'

'Because, if the little lady'd like a lift…'

The man laughed and drove on. Lucienne slunk back into the car, racked by emotion. For his part Ravinel was so furious he'd almost forgotten his fear. She may often have treated him as though he were a boy, but that wasn't the same thing as calling him a fool in that tone of voice.

'You can keep a civil tongue in your head. In fact the best thing you can do is to keep your mouth shut altogether. If we're in a tight spot it's your doing just as much as mine.'

Had she really been intending to make off? To walk back to Le Mans, leaving him on the road? As though, by so doing, she could wash her hands of the whole affair!

Lucienne said nothing. She was sulking. It was obvious from her attitude that she wasn't going to lift a finger to help him. He could fend for himself. It wasn't any too easy. To reassemble a carburetor in the dark, with only a flashlight which never threw the light quite where you wanted it. More than once he almost dropped a screw. But, strangely enough, his anger helped him. He had never felt so competent.

At last he got back into his seat and pressed the starter. The engine started and turned over sweetly. He could have driven on then and there, but he didn't. Out he got again, and, taking one of the cans out of the trunk he emptied it into the gas tank. Quite unnecessarily. It was only bravado. And he took his time about it too! With quite leisurely movements he put the empty can away, locked up the trunk, and got back into the car.

It was half past twelve when he let in the clutch. He drove fast. Not so much on account of the delay as because of a new feeling inside him. He was not far from being delighted. Lucienne had been scared. Not as she had been in the bathroom earlier. This was quite different, real panic. Why? The risks were much the same all along. Anyhow, whatever the reason, something had suddenly changed in their relations. It was she who had quailed. And he wouldn't let her forget it. Not that he would ever refer to it openly. He would just give her a meaning look when she spoke in her domineering voice.

They overtook an oil truck. They were now crossing the rich Beauce corn-lands. The sky had cleared and was now dotted with stars. What had she been thinking about when she had snatched up her bag? About her skin? About her career, her position in the world? For of course she had a position! Sufficient at any rate to enable her to despise him when she felt like it. A traveling salesman! Oh yes. He'd know it for a long time. He was considered a good enough man in his way, but not very subtle. Wasn't he? Perhaps a lot more than he was given credit for!

Nogent-le-Rotrou. An endless, winding, echoing street. A little bridge over a sheet of black water. A notice *Attention—École*, but Ravinel ignored it. There were no schools at night. He swept up the slope which led back onto the plateau. The engine was purring beautifully.

Nom de Dieu! Gendarmes. Three or four of them. A Citroën drawn up diagonally half barring the road. Motorcycles standing on the grass shoulder. The whole scene was as flat as a picture, bathed in the crude glare of his lights which made everything look a bit yellow—the faces, the shoulder-belts and even the boots. Arms were waved. There was nothing for it but to stop. Once again, as in the bathroom, he felt like being sick. He put the brake on hard, automatically, throwing Lucienne forward. She groaned. When he switched off his headlights everything went dark except a flashlight which was trained, first on the hood, then onto their faces. A head surmounted by a kepi peered in through the window. The gendarme's eyes were only a few inches from Ravinel's.

'Where are you from?'

'Nantes… Traveling salesman.'

Ravinel hadn't lost his head. Traveling salesman sounded respectable. Perhaps it might save him.

'Did you overtake a medium-sized van somewhere near Le Mans?'

'I might easily have. But, you know, one doesn't notice.'

The gendarme's eyes inspected Lucienne. As naturally as could be, Ravinel asked:

'Gangsters?'

The gendarme threw a cursory glance into the back of the car, then switched off his flashlight.

'They're carrying an illicit still. The excisemen are on their track.'

'A funny trade to choose,' said Ravinel. 'I'd sooner have mine any day.'

The gendarme moved off and Ravinel slowly drove past the row of men. Not till he was comfortably past did he accelerate.

'That time, I thought we'd had it,' he muttered.

'So did I.'

Her voice was hardly recognizable.

'Of course they may have taken my number.'

'And then?'

It didn't matter. Not in the least. It wasn't part of the plan to conceal that nocturnal journey. In a way, it would be just as well if his number had been taken. If necessary, the gendarme could give evidence that… Still, there was one snag—the presence of a woman in the car. But would the gendarme be likely to remember a detail like that?

The clock on the dashboard moved on patiently. Three o'clock. Four. The lights of Chartres were far behind to the southwest. They were approaching Rambouillet. The night was as dark as ever. That had been taken into account in fixing the date. But there was much more traffic about now. Milk trucks, peasants with handcarts, a mail truck. Ravinel had no time now for thinking. He watched his road with hard eyes. Versailles. Some street cleaners about; otherwise the town was still asleep. Ravinel's shoulders sagged with fatigue. He was thirsty.

Ville-d'Avray… Saint-Cloud… Puteaux… Buildings everywhere, but still no lights in them. Lucienne hadn't budged since the gendarme incident. She wasn't asleep. She simply stared straight in front of her through the misty windshield.

Another stretch of black water—the Seine. And soon the first villas on the outskirts of Enghien. Ravinel's house was near the lake at the end of a little dead-end street. As he turned into it, he went into neutral, switched off the engine, and let the car glide noiselessly, on its own momentum, to its destination. When he got out, his hands were so stiff he fumbled with his keys. Having unlocked the gate, he pushed the car in and hastily closed it again. The house was on the right, on the left, the squat well-built garage which looked more like a little fort. A sloping path led past a clump of bushes to a low shed.

When Lucienne stepped out of the car she staggered and only steadied herself by clutching at the handle of the door. So stiff was she that she had to flex her knees one after the other to bring her legs into action. She had the sulky, forbidding look on her face which belonged to her black moods. Ravinel was already opening one of the rear doors of the car.

'Lend me a hand.'

The bundle was intact, except for one corner where a shoe was visible. The leather had buckled in the water. Ravinel took one end, Lucienne the other.

'Ready?'

She nodded, and together, with bent backs, they carried the thing down the path which, beyond the clump of bushes, was flanked by a row of espalier pear trees. The shed was really a washhouse or *lavoir*. A tiny stream entered at one end and broadened into an artificial pool which was maintained at a fair depth by a dam. Running down to the edge of the pool was an inclined board on which the clothes could be scrubbed. After passing over the dam in a miniature waterfall, the stream flowed on in a wide curve down to the lake.

'The flashlight.'

Lucienne took command once more. The bundle was unrolled on the tiled floor of the lavoir. Lucienne did the work while he held up the light. The body rolled over, a shapeless mass of wet, crumpled clothing. The hair had dried somewhat. Beneath it Mireille's features were twisted into a horrible grimace. It only needed a push now. The body rolled onto the inclined board, slid down it, and splashed into the pool. With her foot, Lucienne gave it a jab to make it sink.

She then gathered up the canvas, groping in the dark, as Ravinel had already switched off the flashlight. It was twenty past five.

'I've just got time,' she muttered.

They went into the house and hung up Mireille's hat and coat in the hall. Her handbag they left on the dining-room table.

'Hurry up,' urged Lucienne whose cheeks had regained a little color. 'The Nantes express is at six four. I mustn't miss it on any account.'

When they got back into the car, Ravinel had for the first time the feeling that he was a widower.

FIVE

Ravinel walked slowly down the steps of the Gare Montparnasse. At the entrance to the station he bought a pack of cigarettes. Then he went over to Dupont's. *Chez Dupont tout est bon.* That's what the neon sign said in sickly pink letters, glaring through the wet dawn. Through the windows he could see a row of backs at the long bar, on which stood an enormous percolator with all sorts of valves, handles, and gauges, which a waiter was polishing, yawning as he worked. Ravinel chose a seat behind the door, sat down and tried to relax. It wasn't the first time he'd been there at that hour. Far from it. Again and again, after driving through the night, he had made a detour and stopped there so as not to get home too early and wake Mireille up. It seemed just the same today, only…

'Black, please. And three croissants.'

He felt like a convalescent. He was conscious of his ribs, of his elbows, of his knees, of every muscle. At the slightest movement a wave of fatigue went through him. His head seemed to be packed with some hot, throbbing substance which pressed on his eyeballs and drew the skin taut over the bones of his face. He was tempted to go to sleep then and there in the warm steamy atmosphere of the café. But he mustn't. For the most difficult part was still to be done. He had to discover the body.

This overpowering sleepiness—he hadn't bargained for that. Yet he saw that it might serve his purpose. Everyone would think that he was stunned with grief. He got his money ready on the table, then dipped one of the croissants into the coffee, which had a nasty acrid taste, like bile. Thinking things over, he decided that the gendarme incident was quite unimportant. Even if the man remembered that there was a woman in the car, there was an easy answer. A hitchhiker. A woman he didn't know from Eve. She had thumbed a ride as he was leaving Angers, and he had put her down at Versailles. No one could possibly connect her with Mireille. And who would think of inquiring about a woman passenger on the early morning train to Nantes?

Even if she came under suspicion for a moment, they'd go no further than checking her alibi at the estimated time of death. As for Ravinel, he had been in Nantes all the time, and he could bring forward twenty or thirty persons to prove it. His movements could be verified almost to the hour. There wasn't a single gap long enough to matter.

Wednesday, November 4th. The post-mortem would certainly establish the date and no doubt make a fairly accurate guess at the time. Wednesday, the 4th. What had he done? Passed the evening at the Brasserie de la Fosse. And the next morning… But what was the point of going over all that? That's what Lucienne had said when they parted.

They were bound to find it was an accident. A sudden attack of giddiness. Mireille had fallen into the stream. There was the question of her clothes, of course. That wasn't so good. A woman doesn't do her washing dressed for going out. But she didn't need to be washing. There are plenty of other reasons for going into a lavoir. To bring in some clothes that had been hanging up to dry, for instance. In any case nobody was going to probe that far. And if they preferred to regard it as suicide, he'd no objection. The two years were up. The insurance company couldn't refuse to pay.

Ten to seven. Time to be going. He couldn't face the last croissant. The other two had been difficult enough. On the pavement, he hesitated. Cars and buses were streaming in all directions. Crowds of workmen and clerks from the suburbs were pouring out of the station. The shuffle of feet, the sound of tires. A nasty day, with a low, leaden sky. The desolate look of early-morning Paris.

Come on! He'd got to go through with it.

The car was parked near the ticket office, outside which was displayed a huge map of France, showing the railway network. It was like an open hand, with lines running radially from the center. Paris-Bordeaux, Paris-Toulouse, Paris-Nice. Life lines, fate lines. Life, fortune, destiny... But meanwhile there was a job to be done! Ravinel tore himself away, backed the car out, and drove off, mentally running through all the things that had to be seen to. He must notify the insurance company as soon as possible. He must send a telegram to Mireille's brother, Germain. Then there'd be the funeral. No higgledy-piggledy affair—Mireille wouldn't have liked that. He was driving like an automaton. He knew every street by heart, and there wasn't yet much traffic about... She wasn't what you'd call religious, Mireille, but she used to go to church all the same. To High Mass, generally, for she liked the music. Besides, people wore their best clothes, and she liked that too. And during Lent she never missed one of Father Riquet's sermons over the radio. Even when she didn't quite understand what he was saying, she could always enjoy

75

his beautiful diction. And then, he'd been in a concentration camp…

The Porte de Clignancourt. A glow of pink in the east—the sun was trying to pierce through the clouds… Suppose there was such a thing as the soul, after all. Suppose the dead could look down on us… If Mireille did that, she'd know he hadn't acted from malice. No, that was ridiculous! And to think that he hadn't got a single black suit to wear! He'd have to get one dyed. Meanwhile he could get one of the neighbors to sew a crêpe band on his sleeve. So many things to think about! And there was Lucienne calmly waiting at Nantes. It wasn't fair… Ravinel stopped thinking, as he was having trouble with an old Peugeot just ahead of him which wouldn't let him pass. By the time he'd succeeded in getting by, he was at Epinay and he had to slow down.

'Remember! You've just arrived from Nantes and you don't know your wife's dead,' he said to himself. That was the most difficult thing of all. *He didn't know*…

Enghien. He stopped at a tobacconist's.

'Good morning, Morin.'

'Good morning, Monsieur Ravinel. A bit late today, aren't you? It's generally earlier than this when I see you pass.'

'Held up by the fog. Quite thick at Angers.'

'Can't think how you do it—driving all through the night.'

'You soon get used to it… Give me a box of matches. Anything been happening here?'

'Good heavens no. Nothing ever happens at Enghien.'

Ravinel left the shop. It couldn't be put off any longer now. If only he hadn't been all alone! How much easier it would have been if… Hallo! There was old Goutre. That was a stroke of luck.

'How are you these days, Monsieur Ravinel?'

'So-so. Jogging along. But I'm glad I've run into you. I was wanting to see you.'

'What can I do for you?'

'It's that lavoir of ours. I'm worried about it. One day it's going to fall on our heads.'

'What? That shed at the end of your garden?'

'Yes. If you've got a moment to spare you might have a look at it now. Only last weekend, my wife was saying—'

'The thing is, I've got to get to the yard.'

'Come on. The yards can wait for you. And we'll have a glass of Muscadet. There's nothing like starting the day on Muscadet. And I've some pretty good stuff. I get it direct from the grower, who's a friend of mine.'

Goutre allowed himself to be persuaded. He got into the car.

'But I mustn't be long. Tailhade's waiting for me…'

They had only a few hundred yards to go, past villas of fussy architecture. Nothing was said. When Ravinel drew up in front of Le Gai Logis he gave a toot on his horn.

'Don't get out. My wife'll come and open the gate.'

'She may not be up yet.'

'At this time of day? Go on! Most of all on a Saturday.'

He tried to smile, gave another long toot.

'The shutters are still closed,' remarked Goutre.

Ravinel got out of the car. 'Mireille!' he called.

Goutre got out too.

'Funny! I told her I was coming. I always let her know when I can.'

Ravinel opened the gate. The clouds were thinning out, leaving transient streaks of blue.

'St. Martin's summer,' sneered Goutre.

Then he added:

'You're letting your gate rust, Monsieur Ravinel. It badly needs a coat of red lead.'

A newspaper was stuck halfway into the mailbox that was perched on one of the gateposts. When he pulled it out, a postcard came with it.

'Hallo! Here's my card,' he muttered. 'Mireille can't be here. Must have gone to see her brother. I hope nothing's wrong. He hasn't been in good shape since the war.'

He walked up to the house.

'I'll join you in a moment. Just going to take my things off. You know the way.'

There was a musty smell in the house. He switched on the hall light, which was fitted with a pink silk lampshade that Mireille had made herself, with the aid of instructions she had read in a magazine. Goutre remained standing on the lawn.

'Go on,' Ravinel called out. 'I'll catch up with you.'

He loitered in the kitchen so as to allow Goutre to get there first. He heard him saying:

'Fine endives you've got here. You've got green thumbs all right, I must say.'

Ravinel followed him leaving the front door open. He lit a cigarette to help him keep his composure.

Goutre had already reached the lavoir. He went in, and Ravinel stopped dead, incapable of advancing another step. He could hardly breathe.

'Monsieur Ravinel…'

Goutre was calling him. In vain Ravinel tried to make his legs move. They wouldn't. What was he to do? Shout

78

for help? Burst into tears? Goutre reappeared standing in the doorway.

'I say, have you seen this?'

At last Ravinel's limbs were released. He ran forward. 'What? What is it?'

'Good heavens, you don't need to take it like that. It's not beyond repair. Look at this.'

He led Ravinel in and pointed to a beam. With his foot-rule he scraped the wood and it fell in powder.

'Rotten. Rotten right through. We'll have to take it out altogether and put a new rafter in.'

Ravinel stood with his back to the water. He hadn't the courage to turn round and look.

'Yes… I see… Quite rotten…' he stammered lamely.

'Then there's this board…'

Goutre turned. Not so Ravinel. He went on gazing at the roof, the rafters of which seemed now to be turning like a huge wheel. A sickening feeling—he thought he was going to faint.

'The cement's all right,' went on Goutre, quite naturally, 'but the woodwork. What can you expect. Everything wears out in time.'

The fool! With an immense effort Ravinel turned round. He dropped his cigarette. The stream was in front of him, almost at his feet. He could distinctly see the pebbles on the bottom, a rusty hoop of a barrel, a little straggling vegetation, and the edge of the dam over which the water trickled, catching the light as it fell. Bending down, Goutre was sticking the blade of a pocketknife into the wood. When he stood up again, he threw a glance round, and he too looked right down into the pool, at which Ravinel was staring as though hypnotized. It cost him an effort to tear his eyes away. Then he gazed all round him, at the field opposite covered with scanty grass, at the boiler, in front of which some cinders had fallen onto the bare cement floor, the floor on which they had only a couple of hours earlier unrolled the canvas.

'Your cigarette.'

Goutre picked it up and handed it to him. He looked thoughtful and kept tapping his thigh with his foot-rule.

'What I ought to tell you,' he went on, looking up, 'is that you need a new roof altogether. But, as a matter of fact, in your place I'd simply patch the thing up.'

Ravinel was once more staring at the pool. Even admitting that the stream was strong enough to carry the body along—and he wouldn't admit that it was—it couldn't possibly have taken it over the dam. It was no more than a trickle.

'Twenty thousand francs might well see you through. But you were quite right to call me in. It's high time something was done about it. If that was to come down on your good lady's head!... But what's the matter, Monsieur Ravinel? You're looking that queer...'

'Nothing. Just fatigue. I've been driving all night.' Goutre took measurements and made notes on an old envelope with a carpenter's pencil.

'Let's see... Tomorrow's Sunday... Monday I've a job to do at Vérondis'... Tuesday... Will it be all right if I send a man round on Tuesday? I suppose Madame Ravinel will be here.'

'Yes... At least I don't know... Perhaps not... It all depends. I'll drop in on my way and let you know.'

'Right.'

Ravinel would have liked to throw himself down on his bed,

close his eyes and think things out. There must be something to be done. If only he could understand what had happened! It was inconceivable. Absolutely inconceivable. And here was this man at his elbow who calmly filled his pipe, commented on the lettuce, and inspected the pear trees, nodding approvingly.

'What do you treat them with? Smoke? No? You may be making a mistake there. Does them a lot of good. Only yesterday Chaudron was saying to me… No, it wasn't yesterday. It was Thursday…'

Ravinel almost bit through his lips. He would have liked to go down on his knees and beseech Goutre to go away.

'I'll be back in a second.'

He must have one more look at the lavoir, though the place was as bare as a barn. After all there were hallucinations which made you see things that weren't there. Why shouldn't there be others which had the opposite effect, which made you blind to things which were staring you in the face? A bleak ray of sunshine was now shining right into the lavoir, lighting up the bottom of the water still more clearly. Yes, he could see every stone, and they looked as though they had never been disturbed. Perhaps they had been to the wrong house and left the body in another lavoir, in all respects identical with this one, in some nightmare country which he would never find again…

Goutre would be getting impatient. Bathed in sweat, Ravinel hurried up the path. He found the builder sitting in the kitchen, going on with his calculations.

'No hurry, Monsieur Ravinel. I'll get this worked out, now I'm at it. I was thinking of using a concrete beam, but on second thought…'

Ravinel suddenly remembered the Muscadet he had promised the old man. Of course! That's why he was in no hurry to go!

'Wait a moment. I'm just going down to the cellar.'

All right. He'd have his Muscadet. And if he didn't clear out after that, he'd… Ravinel clenched his fists. Suddenly he was seized by something like a spasm. He stopped at the bottom of the stairs. There! In the cellar! But why on earth should Mireille be in the cellar? His nerves must be going to pieces for him to be assailed by an absurd fear like that. He opened the door and switched on the light. Of course there was nothing there. All the same, he didn't linger. Snatching up a bottle, he dashed up again. He couldn't help being clumsy. He slammed the sideboard door after getting out the glasses and banged the bottle against the corner of the table. He couldn't control his muscles and almost broke the neck of the bottle when he drew out the cork.

'Help yourself, Monsieur Goutre. My hands are shaky. It's extraordinary what eight hours' driving can do to you.'

'It'd be a pity to spill any,' said Goutre, his eye kindling.

He filled two glasses, slowly, like an expert. Then he rose to his feet to drink his host's health.

'Here's to you, Monsieur Ravinel. And to Madame Ravinel too. I certainly hope your brother-in-law isn't ill. Though with this damp weather… It catches me in the leg.'

Ravinel drained his glass at a go. Then he filled it up, drank, and filled it up again.

'You certainly know how to put it down!'

'When I'm tired like this… Brings me back to life.'

'I should think so! This stuff would bring a corpse back to life!'

Ravinel caught hold of the table. His head really was going round this time.

'Excuse me, Monsieur Goutre. But I'm afraid I've got a good deal to do. You don't mind my being frank, do you?'

Goutre put on his cap.

'That's all right. In any case I'd have to be going.'

He tilted the bottle to read the label. *Muscadet Supérieur—Basse-Goulaine.*

'You can give my compliments to the chap that produces that stuff. He certainly knows his business.'

There were still a few polite exchanges to be gone through at the front door. Then at last Ravinel was alone. He shut the door and locked it, dragged himself back into the kitchen and tossed off the remains of the bottle.

'Inconceivable!' he kept muttering.

His mind seemed to be perfectly clear, but with the clarity of dreams. You see a wall. You touch it. You know it's a wall. Yet that doesn't stop your walking clean through it. You feel the plaster going through your body, and it seems quite natural. The clock on the mantelpiece ticked away busily, reminding him of that other one in the room at Nantes.

'Inconceivable.'

Ravinel shook himself and went into the dining room. Mireille's bag was still on the table. Nor had her coat and hat moved from the hall. He went upstairs. The house was empty, completely empty. All at once he realized that he was holding the bottle by the neck, as though it were a mace. He was scared, terrified to the marrow of his bones. He put the bottle down on the floor, very quietly, as though from now on no sound were permissible. It was with the utmost care that he opened the drawer of his bureau in which his revolver was kept. It was there all right, wrapped in a greasy cloth. He wiped it, pulled the trigger to bring a live round opposite the barrel. At the click he swung round. Instinctively. He couldn't help it. What was the matter with him? What had he expected to see? And this revolver—what was the good of it? Can you shoot down a ghost? He sighed and slipped the gun into his trouser pocket. It was absurd, of course, but it was reassuring to have it there. He sat down on the bed, his hands clasped between his knees. Where was he to begin?

Mireille's body was no longer there. It was a fact, and he was beginning to accept it as such. It wasn't in the pool, it wasn't in the lavoir, it wasn't in the house, it wasn't… But wait a moment! What about the garage?

He rushed downstairs and opened the garage. Nothing there. Nothing, that is to say, except a few cans of oil and some black greasy rags. Then he had another idea and walked slowly towards the lavoir studying the path. He could make out his own footprints and Goutre's too. No one else's. What did that prove? What had been in his mind? He no longer knew. He was at the mercy of sudden impulses, feeling the need to do something. But what? He looked round him despairingly. On either hand were empty building plots. His closest neighbors could see no more than the frontage of the Gai Logis. Should he call on them? Should he go round to all the neighbors to see what he could find out?

He drifted back to the kitchen. What should he say to them if he did?

'I say! I've killed my wife. You haven't by any chance come upon the body? I've mislaid it!'

Farcical, wasn't it?

If only he could have got hold of Lucienne, but she was still in the train. He couldn't telephone to her before twelve. Should he go back to Nantes himself? On what pretext? Supposing the body was discovered somewhere during the course of the day—how could he explain his flight? For that's what it would look like.

It was a vicious circle. He couldn't do anything until he knew what had happened. But how could he find out if he did nothing? Ravinel looked at the clock. Five past ten. Normally he should have called on his firm, Blache et Lehuédé in the Boulevard Magenta. And that was the best thing he could do. So, after carefully shutting up the house, he got into his car again and drove back towards Paris. It was fine now. The air was fresh, but with no bite in it, in fact it was more like an early spring day than a November one. An open car passed him heading for the country, its occupants bareheaded, their hair flying in the wind. At the sight of them, Ravinel felt weak, old, and guilty. He thought of Mireille and he couldn't help a feeling of resentment. She had let him down. And, besides that, she had succeeded where he had always failed: she had crossed the mysterious frontier, she was on the other side, invisible, elusive, and it gave her an unfair advantage. She had seized it to put a spoke in his wheel. Was it possible to be alive and dead at the same time? He had always felt, obscurely, that it was… All the same, her body must be somewhere…

His ideas became confused. He was half asleep. It was really some other self that was coolly and competently driving the car, recognizing every turning, and in the end it was as though the car, not he, chose to stop at the right place in the Boulevard Magenta.

From the Boulevard Magenta, the car took him on into the center, stopping outside a small café-restaurant in the neighborhood of the Louvre. It was a quarter he never frequented, but today he wasn't altogether master of his movements. He was making a mental calculation in which he kept on getting the times wrong.

Lucienne's train got in at eleven twenty. Or was it eleven forty? No, that was impossible: the journey took five hours. Five hours from six four. That made it eleven four. The hospital was no more than five minutes from the station, so she must be there by now. He went into the restaurant.

'Lunch, Monsieur?'

'Oh. If you like…'

The waiter stared at this unshaven customer who ran his hand over his eyes. Had a night out, perhaps.

'The telephone?'

'At the far end on the right.'

'Can I make a long-distance call?'

'See the girl at the cash desk, will you?'

The telephone was by the door to the kitchen, which was never shut for more than five seconds at a time, and, as he stood there, Ravinel was conscious of a constant volley of orders behind his back.

'Three hors-d'oeuvres. And isn't that entrecôte ready yet?'

There were wheezings on the line and Lucienne's voice was hardly recognizable. It sounded far away, terribly far. And with all the row and bustle behind him…

'Lucienne!… Can you hear me?… Yes, it's Fernand speaking… She's gone… No, they haven't come to fetch her—she's gone, disappeared. When I got back there was no sign of her.'

Someone was standing near him waiting to take his place, filling in the time by combing his hair at the mirror over the washbasin.

'Are you there, Lucienne?… You must come back… What?… A confinement? To hell with the confinement… No, I'm not ill. Nor drunk either! I know perfectly well what I'm saying… Not a trace… What? You don't imagine that I'm inventing it just to make you come back?… What?… Of course I should have preferred it. But if it's absolutely impossible to come straight away… All right, then. Tomorrow at twelve forty… Go back and have another look? Where do you want me to look?… Of course I don't understand any more than you do… Very well, then. Tomorrow.'

Ravinel rang off and chose a seat by the window. He couldn't blame Lucienne. If someone had telephoned the news to him, would he have believed it? He waded through the meal absent-mindedly, then got back into the car. Once again the Porte de Clignancourt, then the road to Enghien. Of course he must get back to the house. Lucienne was quite right about that. He'd even have another look round. Just in case. And he'd better be seen by the neighbors. The thing was to gain time. And to behave as though he had nothing on his conscience.

He opened the front door. Everything was exactly as he had left it. He was vaguely disappointed. Why? What was he expecting?

As a matter of fact he expected nothing. His mind no longer looked forward into the future. All he wanted was peace, quiet, and forgetfulness. Going upstairs, he put his revolver down on the bedside table. To make sleep doubly sure, he took a pill. Then without stopping to undress he threw himself down on the bed. In half a minute he was sound asleep.

SIX

It was nearly five when he woke up, limbs stiff, stomach heavy, face puffy, hands clammy. But when he asked himself where the body could have got to, the answer came in a flash:

'It's been stolen.'

For some reason, this answer was consoling, and, as he washed and shaved, he was relatively calm.

'That's what it is. Someone's pinched it.'

That was serious enough. Indeed it was very serious. But the danger was of a different sort. You can come to terms with a thief. He has his price.

The last wisps of sleep were brushed from his head. Once more he was in contact with his surroundings, the rooms, the furniture. His legs felt better. The stiffness soon wore off and he strode about firmly, purposefully. The house seemed friendly and familiar now. No mystery about it. Things weren't so bad, after all. So long as he kept his head… The body had been stolen: with that once accepted…

But the more closely he looked at the idea, the more difficult it was to accept. Steal a corpse? Why should anyone want to? And what a frightfully risky business for the thief. As regards his neighbors, he knew them pretty well. On the right as you faced the street was Bigaux, a railway clerk of fifty. A conscientious, dull little man who knew his place, and kept it. His work, his garden, his family, his game of belote of

89

an evening—that was his world. Bigaux hiding a corpse! The idea was unthinkable. And his wife had a gastric ulcer. A flimsy creature you could knock down with a feather. On the other side, Poniatowski, who was in the accounts department of a furniture factory. Divorced. Hardly ever there. It was said that he wanted to sell the place…

In any case neither Bigaux nor Poniatowski could have witnessed the scene that morning. Admittedly they could have gone into the lavoir afterwards, but not without trespassing. And what was the use of a body if you didn't know who'd committed the crime? For there was only one conceivable reason for wanting it—blackmail. Even then, nobody knew about the insurance policy, and that was the one thing that could make blackmail worth while. A traveling salesman isn't a capitalist. Everyone knew that Ravinel made a decent living—no more. Admittedly there were blackmailers who were patient men and squeezed you slowly drop by drop over a long period. But that needed a lot of nerve. Who else was there? A passer-by? A burglar?… To steal a corpse on the spur of the moment was enterprising, to say the least!

As theory after theory passed through his mind, he became once more overwhelmed by a sensation of helplessness. After a while he decided that the body hadn't been stolen after all. But it wasn't there. So it must have been. But nobody could possibly want to steal it…

And so it went on, round and round in a circle. Ravinel felt a little pain beneath his left temple and rubbed the spot. No question of his falling ill at this juncture. He simply hadn't the right to! But what was he to do, *Bon Dieu*, what was he to do?

He wandered about the room, biting his lips, crushed by an overpowering sense of loneliness. He hadn't the energy even to straighten the crumpled counterpane, let the dirty water away from the washbasin, or pick up the empty bottle. Instead, he merely kicked it under the wardrobe. Taking his revolver, he went downstairs. Where should he go? He looked out of the front door. It was getting dark, though streaks of pink still trailed across the western sky. An airplane flew overhead. A dreary, mournful evening. Like the one on which he'd first met Mireille on the Quai des Grands-Augustins, where the second-hand booksellers have their queer little stalls perched on the parapet. He was fingering some volumes. And there she was, turning over the pages of a book. The lights were going on one after the other. They could hear the whistle of the policeman at the bridge. It was silly to recall such things. They hurt.

Ravinel went to the lavoir. The water still trickled quietly over the dam, making little bubbles which caught the red of the sunset. A goat bleated in the field on the other bank of the stream. It belonged to the postman. Something clicked in Ravinel's brain. The postman's goat! Every morning his young daughter led it into the field and tethered it to a stake. Every evening she came to fetch it. Was it possible that?…

The postman was a widower and there was no other child. The girl was called Henriette. She was generally at home. To tell the truth, she was a bit simple-minded. Not that she was an idiot. Far from it. She did the housework and the cooking and acquitted herself pretty well for a girl of twelve.

'I wonder if you could tell me something, Mademoiselle.'

Nobody had ever called her Mademoiselle before, and she was too intimidated to think of asking him in. For that matter, so was he. He was out of breath from running, and he was uncertain how he ought to begin.

'Did you take the goat into the field this morning?' he ventured. The girl reddened, instantly alarmed.

'What has she done?'

'I live just across the stream—the Gai Logis. The lavoir belongs to me.'

She squinted slightly and he studied each of her eyes in turn, on the lookout for any sign of lying.

'My wife left some handkerchiefs hanging up to dry. They must have been blown away.'

It was an absurd pretext, but he was too tired to think up anything better.

'You didn't see them lying about or floating in the stream, did you?'

She had a long narrow face. A plait of hair fell on either side. Even with her mouth shut, two teeth protruded. Ravinel felt vaguely that there was something pathetic in this interview.

'You picketed the goat quite close to the stream. You didn't look at the lavoir, did you?'

'Yes. I did.'

'Try and remember. Was there anything?'

'No. I didn't notice anything.'

'At what time were you there?'

'I don't know.'

A sizzling noise came from the end of the passage. She reddened still more and squirmed.

'That's the soup boiling over. May I go and see?'

'Of course. Run quick.'

She darted off, and now that the way was no longer barred he went indoors. He didn't want the neighbors to see him there. He had a glimpse of the kitchen. Some clothes were hanging up to dry. He ought to have gone. It didn't seem right to try and pump this child.

'It was the soup,' she said when she returned. 'It boiled over.'

'Is much gone?'

'Not a lot. I dare say my father won't notice.'

Her nose was a bit pinched. And she had a few freckles, like Mireille.

'Does he scold you?' asked Ravinel.

He regretted the question at once, realizing that this girl was experienced far beyond her years. He went on hurriedly:

'At what time do you get up?'

She frowned, tugged at one of her plaits. Perhaps she was looking for her words.

'Was it dark when you got up this morning?'

'Yes.'

'And you took the goat out right away.'

'Yes.'

'Perhaps you walked it about the field a bit before tying it up?'

'No.'

'Why not?'

She wiped her mouth with the back of her hand. Turning her head away, she muttered: 'I'm afraid.'

At twelve he'd been afraid of the dark himself. Often he'd had to walk to school before daylight, and he'd been unable to shake off the feeling someone was following him. Even in the street. If he'd been asked to take a goat out into the fields it would have been worse… He looked at Henriette's face. Yes, it was already old, worn by fears and responsibilities. And in his mind's eye he saw the budding Fernand Ravinel, that boy nobody had ever talked to him about, and about whom he didn't care to think, that boy who had nevertheless followed him through life, who was a witness…

He could find nothing more to say. He hadn't the heart to probe further. Supposing that boy of twelve had found a corpse floating on the water…

No. That was something he couldn't ask, and it was left as a sort of secret between these two.

He nevertheless forced himself to ask a few more questions:

'You didn't see anybody in the field?'

'No. I don't think so.'

'Nor in the lavoir?'

'No.'

He put his hand in his pocket, but all he found was a ten-franc piece. All the same he put it in her hand.

'That's for you.'

'He'll take it from me.'

'Nonsense. You can find somewhere to hide it.'

She shook her head pensively. She took the coin nevertheless.

'I'll come and see you again,' promised Ravinel.

He felt he must leave on a buoyant, optimistic note. As though there had never been any question of goats or lavoirs. As Ravinel left, he ran into the postman, who carried his bag of letters in front of him with something of the carriage of a pregnant woman.

'Good evening, Monsieur Ravinel. Came to see me, did you? About your special delivery, I expect.'

94

'No. At least… As a matter of fact I'm expecting a registered letter. A special delivery, you said?'

The other was scrutinizing him from under the cracked peak of his kepi.

'Yes. I rang. And then, as there was no answer, I shoved it into the mailbox. Is your wife away?'

'She's gone to Paris.'

There was no reason why he should answer, but he did so humbly, feeling he had to placate everybody.

'*Salut!*' said the postman taking his leave.

And he went in and shut the door.

A special delivery! It couldn't have come from the firm, as he'd called there that morning. From Germain? That wasn't likely either. Unless it was addressed to Mireille.

He hurried home through the lighted streets. It was almost cold all of a sudden and that seemed to clear his brain. The postman's daughter hadn't seen anything. If she had, she hadn't understood. Or, if she had understood, she would keep quiet about it.

But, to come back to that special delivery, it might be from the thief, dictating his terms.

It was there all right in the box, tilted up on one corner. He took it indoors and looked at the envelope under the kitchen light.

Monsieur Fernand Ravinel

That handwriting! If it wasn't…

He shut his eyes and counted ten. He must be ill, seriously ill. Then he opened them and looked at the envelope again. No!

It was no use saying it was Mireille's writing. It wasn't. Because it couldn't be. It was absolutely impossible.

The envelope was carefully stuck up, right to the corners. He needed a pointed instrument to open it, and took the carving knife out of a drawer. With it in his hand he walked menacingly back to the table, on which the mauve envelope was lying. It was difficult, however, to insert even the point of the knife and finally, losing patience, Ravinel tore the thing open roughly. He read the note right through without understanding a word.

> *Darling*
>
> *I've got to go away for two or three days. It's nothing serious, so don't be alarmed. I'll explain it all later. Meanwhile you'll find plenty to eat in the refrigerator in the cellar. Finish up the old pot of jam before opening a fresh one, and remember to turn off the gas when you've finished with the oven. You so easily forget.*
>
> *Love and kisses to my big bad wolf*
>
> *Mireille*

Ravinel read it a second time, then a third. Suddenly he had it—it had been delayed in the post. The letter itself was undated, but the post mark on the envelope was quite legible. *Paris. 7 Nov. 1600 hrs.*

The 7th of November. That would be… Good heavens—today!

He had read somewhere of split personalities and their capacity for banishing things from their minds. Very well! So could he! Mireille was in Paris—what could be more natural? And she'd handed the letter in at four o'clock…

Something gripped him by the throat. He laughed savagely—a laugh that was more like a retching. Tears clouded his eyes. And suddenly he hurled the carving knife across the room with all his strength. It came to rest, quivering like an arrow, the point deep in the door. With open mouth and distorted features he stared at it for a moment. Then everything swam round him, the floor gave way beneath his feet and he fell heavily, his head striking the tiles.

As he lay there motionless a trickle of thick saliva oozed from the corner of his mouth.

When he came to, after what must have been a long time, his first thought was that he was dying, his second that he was already dead. He felt lighter than air, floating. Then little by little two parts of him seemed to separate like oil and water, forming different layers. On one level he felt delivered, a sensation of infinite relief; on the other he felt bogged down and hopelessly entangled. It seemed to him that with a little effort he could break through some thin partition and open his eyes on to another world. But he couldn't; his eyes were no longer under his control.

Then suddenly he was conscious of a vast, colorless expanse. It wasn't paradise, nor purgatory either. Call it the shades. At all events he was free at last. And he was intact. No, that was putting it badly, for he was like some infinitely malleable substance that can be molded into any shape. A soul. Yes, that's what he was—a soul. And as such he could make a fresh start. Start what? Never mind about that: the question was quite unimportant. What mattered was to take stock of this great white expanse, to surrender himself to it, let himself be impregnated by it, till he became white and luminous too. To become pure, pure as water.

And now the white space became tinged with gold. Indeed it was no longer space—at least not empty space. It was divided into different zones and some were darker than others, and from one of them came a regular mechanical sound, probably coming from the world, the old world, the one he had left. And something was moving—a small black dot in the middle of a stretch of white. What was it? There must be a word for it, for, after all, everything had a name. If only he could find it! With that word, the frontier would be crossed once and for all. The peace he felt would no longer be precarious. It would become an eternal tranquil joy, mixed with a touch of melancholy. There it was. It was coming now—the word. It was forming, deep down, and slowly rising to the surface. Soon it would be there. Why should that suddenly seem menacing?

Fly.

A fly. Yes it was a fly, a fly crawling across the ceiling. And this dark splodge on his right was the cupboard. Bit by bit everything was starting again. In cold and silence... I feel round me. A tiled floor. I'm cold. I'm lying down. I'm Fernand Ravinel... And there's a letter on the table...

Better not go into that. Don't ask questions, don't try to find out. Hold on to oblivion. So long as you do, you won't care. That's the important thing: not to care. But it's hard, it's exhausting... Don't think about it. Just try your limbs to see if they work.

They did. The muscles obeyed him. His arm moved, his hand was capable of grasping. His eyes fell on things and knew them. His brain found words to call them by. He could stand… But on the table—That bit of paper and that envelope—he mustn't see them, he mustn't find words for them. They were too dangerous, much too dangerous.

He must turn his back on them. He lurched to the front door, went out, and slammed it behind him. There! That was better. He locked the door. Better still. No one could say now what was behind it. He mustn't know. He mustn't ever see that letter again, or anything might happen. The words might leave the page and form themselves into fantastic threatening shapes.

Ravinel was almost at the end of the street before he looked back. The house seemed inhabited, as he'd left the lights on. Often, when he came home of an evening, he would see Mireille's shadow as she crossed behind one of the slatted shutters. But he was too far off now. Even if she passed, he wouldn't be able to see her. He walked to the station. He was bareheaded. In the refreshment room he drank two glasses of beer. Victor, the waiter, was busy at the bar; otherwise he'd have been only too ready for a chat. As it was, he merely gave Ravinel an occasional wink or a smile.

How could cold beer burn your throat like spirits? Ought he to take to flight? What would be the use? Another mauve envelope might come, this one addressed to the police inspector, reporting the crime. Yes, Mireille might lodge a complaint for having been killed! Come on! None of that! Those thoughts were forbidden.

Quite a crowd of people on the station platform. The colored lights were painful. The red signal light was too red, the green one sickeningly sweet. The bookstall smelt of fresh ink. In the train, the people exuded an odor of game and the carriages smelt like those of the underground.

It had to finish like this. Sooner or later he had been bound to discover what was concealed from other beings—that there was no real distinction between the living and the dead. It's only because of the coarseness of our perception that we imagine the dead elsewhere, in some other world. There isn't any other world. Not a bit of it. The dead are with us here, mixed up in our lives and meddling with them. *Remember to turn the gas off when you've finished with the oven…* They speak to us with shadowy mouths; they write with hands of smoke. Ordinary people, of course, don't notice. They're too preoccupied with their own affairs. To perceive these things you've got to have been incompletely born and thus only half involved in this noisy, colorful, flamboyant world…

Yes, he was beginning to understand. That letter was the first step in a process of initiation. Why should he be so frightened about it?

'Tickets, please!'

The ticket collector was a stout, florid man with two rolls of fat at the back of his neck. Many of the passengers were standing, and he brushed past them impatiently. Little did he know that he was at the same time pushing his way through a host of shadows. It wouldn't be long, no doubt, before Mireille was among them. Her letter had been written to prepare him. Thoughtful of her. *It's nothing serious, so don't he alarmed.* Of course not. Nothing serious about death. A change of weight and consistency, that was all. She wasn't unhappy, Mireille. She would explain it all. She said so. Not that there was a great deal to explain. For the most part, he already understood…

Yes, he understood a lot of things all of a sudden. His childhood, for instance. The others, his father, his mother, his friends, had all tried to get him entangled, rooted. School, university, exams, jobs—so many snares to get him caught. Even Lucienne was no different. Money. That was all she thought about: money. As though money wasn't just another load to carry on your shoulders! And the heaviest of all!

For a practice at Antibes, she might answer. But that didn't make any difference: she was out for money all the time. What was the practice for if not to bring in money? They weren't going to Antibes merely to enjoy the sunshine.

Talking of sunshine, that would of course change everything. It would prevent Mireille from appearing. Didn't the sun obliterate the stars? Yet they were there just the same. Antibes! Yes, that really would kill Mireille. It was the only way of killing her. At least, it would wipe her from the scene. Had Lucienne thought of that? Was that why she had picked on Antibes? She generally knew what she was about, that girl…

But now that he had understood, he had no longer the slightest desire to escape to the bright, scintillating south. Of course, if he stayed here, he'd have to overcome his fears. For they were still there, lying doggo for the moment, but only waiting for the right moment to spring at him. It wouldn't be easy. He'd have to face certain memories without flinching— that bathroom at Nantes. Mireille stiff and cold, with her hair plastered down on her forehead.

The train swayed from side to side. The journey seemed endless, but at last he found himself on the platform, jostled by passengers and porters. Outside, it was raining. He went to the nearest post office.

'Give me Nantes, will you?'

The partitions were covered with scribblings—telephone numbers, obscenities.

'Hello! Is that the hospital at Nantes?… I want to speak to Dr. Lucienne Mogard…'

In the telephone booth he could hear no more than a vague murmur of the busy world all round him.

'Hello? Lucienne?… She's written to me. She'll be back in a few days… Who? Mireille of course! Yes, Mireille. She sent me a special delivery… But I tell you she did… No. I'm not out of my mind. And I'm not trying to play on your nerves. I just thought you ought to know… Yes. I realize that. But I've been thinking. And a lot of things—but it would take too long to explain… What am I going to do? How should I know?… All right. See you tomorrow.'

Poor Lucienne! Always wanting to reason things out. All right! Let her try! She'd see for herself. She'd read the letter.

Or could she? Would it be visible to her?… Of course it would. The postman had seen it, hadn't he? He'd spoken about it himself. Obviously it must be a real one. It was only its meaning that was not obvious to every Tom, Dick, and Harry. For you had to be able to think in two worlds at the same time.

Boulevard de Denain. Slanting arrows of luminous rain. The stream of glistening motor cars. Appearances: he knew that now. It was all rather like a café with mirrors all round the walls, till you hardly knew whether you were looking at the real thing or its reflection.

Night flowed down the boulevard like an eddying flood sweeping everything with it, lights, smells, and human beings. Be frank with yourself, Fernand Ravinel: how many times have you not dreamed that you were drowned in this very flood? And if you accepted what was done at Nantes, was it not precisely because it was done *with water?* Have you not always been fascinated by water, beneath whose smooth and brilliant surface is another world that it makes you giddy to think of? Much the same as the fog game, wasn't it? And you wanted Mireille to play it too. Now you are tempted in turn. You envy her, don't you?

Ravinel wandered for a long, long time, not caring where his legs carried him. Coming to the Seine, he trudged along by the side of the stone parapet, which came nearly up to his shoulder. In front of him was a bridge, a far-flung arch beneath which the lights were reflected in oily swirls. The town seemed abandoned. The thin wind smelt of locks and waterways. And Mireille was somewhere, mixed up with the night. They couldn't meet, for they lived on different planes, in different elements. He hadn't yet done the crossing. But they could signal to each other like ships that pass on the trade routes.

'Mireille!'

He spoke the word softly. He couldn't wait any longer. He was in a hurry to cross the frontier too, to smash the mirror.

SEVEN

When he woke up, Ravinel recognized the hotel bedroom. He remembered walking for hours on end. Then he recalled the image of Mireille and heaved a sigh. It took him several minutes, however, to decide that it was probably Sunday. It was indeed certain, because Lucienne was arriving by the twelve-something train. She must already be in the train. What was he to do to fill in the time? What could one do on a Sunday? A dead day, a day on which you could only mark time. And he was in a hurry to forge ahead.

Nine o'clock.

He got up and dressed, then drew back the threadbare curtain that concealed the window. A gray sky. Roofs. A few skylights, some of them still painted blue, a relic of the black-out. Certainly not an inspiring view. Downstairs he paid his bill to an old woman in curlers. It wasn't till he was on the pavement that he realized he was in the neighborhood of the central market, within a stone's throw of where Germain lived.

Why shouldn't he fill in the time there?

Mireille's brother lived in a flat on the fourth floor. A dark staircase. The lights didn't work, and Ravinel had to grope his way up as best he could. Sunday smells. Sunday noises. Behind their doors, people hummed a tune or switched on the wireless, thinking of the afternoon's football game or the movie they'd go to in the evening. On one landing he could hear the hiss of milk boiling over, on another some howling brats. A man with an overcoat slipped on over his pajamas came downstairs leading a dog. It was all very intimate and Ravinel had the feeling of being out of it.

On the fourth floor, he found the key in the door. It was always left there, but Ravinel never took any notice of it. He knocked. It was Germain who came to let him in.

'Why, Fernand! How are you?'

'All right, thanks. And you?'

'Not too good... Excuse the mess: I've only just got up. Now you're here, you'll have a cup of coffee. Yes, yes. Of course you will.'

He led Ravinel into the dining room, pulled out a chair for him, and swept away a dressing gown that was lying there.

'And Marthe?'

'She's gone to church, but she'll soon be back. Sit down, old boy... You're in fine form, Mireille's been telling me. Wish I could say the same of myself... By the way, you haven't seen my latest X-rays. Here, help yourself to some coffee, while I go and fetch them.'

There was a medicinal smell lingering in the air. Eucalyptus mixed with something else. And near the coffeepot was a little saucepan with a hypodermic syringe in it and some needles. What a bore! He wished he hadn't come. Germain was pottering about in the bedroom, occasionally shouting out something to his brother-in-law.

'You'll see. They're beauties. As the doctor says, with proper treatment...'

When you marry you think you're marrying a wife, but you're really marrying a family. That at any rate was what it seemed like to Ravinel. He'd married Germain's germs, Germain's private worries, Germain's experiences as a prisoner of war. What a cheat life is. When you're young it makes such wonderful promises, and then…

Germain returned with several large yellow envelopes, which made him look like one of those messengers in ministries who wander about with armfuls of dockets.

'Go on. Take some coffee… It's true, you've very likely had breakfast already. He's the deuce of a fellow, that Dr. Gleize. The way he explains these photos to you. All you can see is a lot of smudges, but he reads them like a book.'

Germain held one of them up to the light.

'You see that mark there over the heart? Yes, that white part in the heart—I'm becoming quite an expert myself, you see!… No. That faint line there. But you can't see it from that distance. Come close…'

This was what Ravinel hated. He didn't want to know how his inside was made. Nor Germain's either! The spectacle of those bits of skeleton which the X-ray revealed produced in him a strange discomfort. Nature had had the good taste to hide certain things and they had much better remain hidden. The eagerness which Germain displayed to turn himself inside out for anybody's inspection had always disgusted him.

'You can see here where it's cicatrized. It's healing splendidly. Of course I've still got to take care, but the signs are encouraging. With the sputum too. I can show you the latest analysis. Where is it now? I suppose Marthe's shoved it away somewhere—she loses everything… Still it doesn't matter: Mireille can tell you…'

'Yes, yes. Of course…'

Lovingly Germain put the photograph back in its envelope, but it was only to take out another, which he gazed at with his head on one side.

'They cost three thousand francs apiece, you know. Fortunately they're going to raise my pension. In any case I wouldn't grudge the money. When a job's done as well as that… He takes ever so much trouble, Dr. Gleize. But then, you see, he's interested. Says I'm quite a case.'

The key had turned in the front door. Good! That was Marthe back from church.

'*Bonjour*, Fernand. Nice of you to have come. We don't see a lot of you.'

Was that a reproach? She was always a little bit tart beneath her sweetness. She took off her hat and carefully folded up her veil. She was always in mourning for someone or other. To tell the truth, she liked black. It was distinguished, dignified.

'Business good?' she asked with a hint of suspicion in her voice.

'Pretty fair. I can't complain.'

She had already slipped on an apron and was clearing the table. Her movements were swift and competent.

'How's Mireille?'

It was Germain who answered.

'She was here just now. Came a few minutes after you'd left for church. I was still in bed.'

'She gets up early in the morning, these days!' commented Marthe.

Ravinel was making a desperate effort to understand.

'What did you say, Germain? Mireille was… here? When?'

Germain was counting out some drops. Ten, eleven, twelve…

He frowned slightly. He wasn't going to be interrupted. Thirteen, fourteen, fifteen.

'When?' he said casually. 'Oh, I suppose it was about an hour ago. Perhaps more…'

'Mireille!'

Germain put the dropper away, wrapped it first in absorbent cotton, then tissue paper. Then he looked up.

'Mireille, yes. What's funny about that?… Good heavens, man, what's the matter with you? Have I said something wrong?'

'Wait a minute,' said Ravinel in a hoarse whisper. 'Are you telling me that Mireille's been here… this morning… that you actually saw her?'

'Of course I saw her. She walked in, just as usual, and kissed me on both cheeks.'

'You're quite sure about that? That she kissed you, I mean…'

'Really, Fernand. I don't see what you're getting at.'

Marthe, who had gone into the next room, came back and stood in the doorway, studying the two men. To cover his confusion Ravinel took a cigarette out of his case.

'I'm afraid you can't smoke,' said Germain. 'Doctor's orders, you know. If you don't mind…'

'Of course not. I'm sorry.'

Ravinel crushed the cigarette between his fingers nervously.

'It's very odd,' he managed to say. 'She didn't say anything to me about it.'

'She wanted to hear about my X-ray.'

'Did she seem… normal?'

'Absolutely.'

'And when she kissed you… Her skin… Did it seem just the same…'

109

'Look here, Fernand. What is the matter? Did you hear that, Marthe? He doesn't seem to believe me.'

Marthe came into the room and Ravinel sensed at once that she knew something. He went cold, like an accused person before his judge.

'When did you get back from Nantes, Fernand?'

'Yesterday. Yesterday morning.'

'And you didn't find her there, did you?'

Her eyes were shining, and her lips seemed thinner than ever.

'No. Mireille wasn't there.'

Marthe nodded.

'Do you think it's that?' muttered Germain.

'I'm sure of it.'

Ravinel could hold himself no longer.

'For the love of God, tell me. What do you know about it? Were you there yesterday morning?'

Germain was nettled.

'You forget I'm ill.'

'You'd better tell him,' said Marthe and she glided noiselessly into the bedroom.

'Tell me what?' asked Ravinel aggressively. 'One might think you'd been hatching some plot.'

'Gently, now,' said Germain. 'Marthe's right. You'd better know. As a matter of fact I ought to have told you when you got engaged to Mireille. But I thought marriage would put everything to rights. The doctor said—'

'Never mind about the doctor, Germain. Get on with the story.'

'I don't like distressing you, Fernand, but the thing is: Mireille was always liable to go off...'

'Off her head?'

'Oh dear no. It was only a quirk. She'd go off, break out.'

Ravinel knew that Marthe was watching him through the doorway. He was stunned.

'What do you mean—break out?'

'She used to run away. Not often. It began when she was about fourteen.'

'You mean she went off with men?'

'No, Fernand, no. Nothing of that sort. You mustn't get it wrong. She just ran away, left home, disappeared. They said it was just a queer streak in her make-up. Seems it happens pretty often round about puberty. Sometimes she took a train. Sometimes she simply walked on till she dropped. We always had to call the police in.'

'What did the neighbors think?' put in Marthe, who was shaking a pillow.

Germain shrugged his shoulders.

'There's something queer in every family, if you only knew. Even in the best... She was terribly upset about it afterwards, poor kid. But she couldn't do anything about it. When the urge came, off she had to go.'

'What's it got to do with?...'

'Can't you see, Fernand? It's the same thing this time. She's got one of her attacks. But there's no need to make it worse than it is. She'll be back in a day or two.'

'It's nonsense,' Ravinel burst out. 'The thing is—'

Germain sighed.

'That's what I expected. You don't believe it. You see, Marthe, he can't take it in.'

She raised her hand as though taking oath.

'It's true, all the same. And, if I'd had any say in it, you'd have known about it from the first. When a person's not quite normal, you never know what may be wrong. Fortunately you've no children. You might have had one with a harelip.'

'Marthe! Really!'

'I know what I'm saying. I've talked to the doctor about it.'

The doctor again! Always the doctor!

'But I can understand your feelings,' went on Marthe. 'To be told a thing like that all of a sudden… And don't think I enjoy talking about Mireille like this. Poor child. It's not her fault. But there it is, she's—'

Ravinel took his head in his hands.

'Stop,' he groaned. 'I'll go out of my mind.'

But she was not to be silenced.

'The moment I came in, I could tell something was amiss. I'm not like Germain: he never notices anything. And, if I'd seen Mireille, I'd have known at once she was not her usual self.'

Ravinel had torn his cigarette to shreds and it now lay in a little heap on the table. He would have liked to seize these two and bang their heads together. He couldn't bear the sympathetic looks they gave him. Mireille make off! As if she was in a condition to run away after lying two days in a tub full of water! Of course it was nonsense. It was a plot. They were up to something and had concocted this story beforehand… No, that wouldn't wash either. Germain was too stupid. He'd have given himself away in a minute.

'How was she dressed?'

Germain thought for a moment.

'I didn't pay any attention to that, and she was standing against the light. But let me see… Yes. I think she had on her gray fur-trimmed coat. And a little hat. I remember thinking that she had rather wintry clothes on for this weather.'

'Perhaps she was going to catch a train,' suggested Marthe.

'Oh no. At least, she didn't give me that impression. But what puzzles me, now I come to think of it, is that she didn't seem in the least excited. Formerly, when she had her attacks, she was always nervy and overwrought, ready to burst into tears at the least thing. While this morning she was as calm as could be.'

And, as Ravinel clenched his fists, he added:

'You know, Fernand, she's a good girl at heart.'

It was twenty past ten by the clock on the mantelpiece, a preposterous gilt affair supported by two nymphs with naked breasts. Lucienne's train would have already passed Le Mans. Marthe pottered about in the room.

'I know what you're thinking,' said Germain.

Ravinel started.

'You think she deceives you, don't you?'

The fool! No, he certainly wasn't pretending.

'But you're making a great mistake if you harbor any suspicions of that sort. I know Mireille. I don't say she's always easy to understand, but there's one thing: she's straight as a die.'

'My poor Germain!' sighed Marthe.

It was obvious what she meant.

'My poor Germain! A lot you know about women!'

Germain bristled.

'Mireille? Go on! She's much too wrapped up in her home. Why, you've only to see her there…'

'She's too much alone,' said Marthe quietly. 'Not that that's any reflection on you, Fernand. You've got your job and you have to travel. That doesn't alter the fact that it's

113

not much fun for a young woman when her husband's hardly ever there…'

'Now, when I was a prisoner of war,' began Germain.

There! The very subject Ravinel always tried to avoid. The mischief was done, however. Once on his favorite topic, there was no stopping Germain, though he'd told every one of his stories at least twenty times before. Ravinel didn't listen. Nor did he think—not really. He simply let himself drift on the tide of a somewhat mournful reverie. In spirit, he was back at Enghien, wandering through the empty house, and if anyone had visited it at that moment he would no doubt have been conscious of a disconsolate shadow in the likeness of Fernand Ravinel.

Germain swore he'd seen her, but weren't there thousands of people to swear they'd seen a ghost? That's what it was. Mireille, dead, had chosen to appear to her brother. She had caught him at a moment when he was still half asleep and not capable of analyzing his own perceptions. He *thought* he saw her. A typical case. He had read of others in the *Revue Métapsychique* which he used to take before his marriage. Besides, what he had just learned about Mireille proved she was psychic. People like that always were. And a psychic person would obviously be just the person to make a ghost.

'What did she say, exactly?' he asked suddenly.

Germain was telling of a brush he'd had with one of the Stalag orderlies. He broke off, a little hurt.

'What did she say?… I really couldn't tell you. For that matter it was I who did most of the talking, since she'd come to inquire about the X-ray.'

'Did she stay long?'

'Only a few minutes.'

'I don't see why she couldn't have waited for me,' complained Marthe.

But that was just the point! If Marthe had been in the flat, Mireille wouldn't have been visible. There was a certain logic even in supernatural things.

'You didn't think of looking out of the window to see which way she went?'

'No. Why should I?'

Quite so. But it was a pity all the same. If he'd looked out of the window he would no doubt have discovered that Mireille never left the building at all. And that would have been an absolute proof.

'You really mustn't get worked up about it,' said Germain. 'Look here, old man. If you want my advice—go back home. You'll very likely find her waiting for you. She may be in a bit of a state about it, but now that you've heard everything you'll know how to handle her.'

He tried to laugh genially. Marthe gave him a reproving glance.

'As a child did she ever walk in her sleep?'

'Not Mireille. I did… I didn't climb up on the roof or anything of that sort, but I used to talk a lot in my sleep and gesticulate, and several times I woke up to find myself in the passage or in another room altogether. A nasty feeling, I can tell you. I used to be so scared I couldn't go back to sleep again.'

'I don't know that there's any need to go into that,' put in Marthe a little sharply, 'though by the look on Fernand's face he seems to be enjoying it.'

'Does it ever happen to you now?' went on Ravinel, ignoring her.

'Come on. Let's drop the subject. What about something to drink before you go? I'm afraid we can't ask you to stay for lunch. You see, I'm on a diet.'

'In any case you ought to go home,' said Marthe decisively. 'You can't leave Mireille all alone.'

Germain got out some liqueur glasses, including one for himself.

'You know what the doctor says about drinking,' Marthe objected.

'Oh. Just a thimbleful.'

Ravinel plucked up all his courage.

'And suppose Mireille isn't there? Suppose she doesn't come back tonight? What do you advise me to do?'

'Nothing. The best thing is to wait. Don't you think so, Marthe? After all, you're not obliged to go back to Nantes tomorrow. A day won't make any difference. And a lot depends on it, you know. If she comes back and finds the house empty, there's no knowing what will happen. Take a few days off and see how things turn out. Meanwhile you can make a few discreet inquiries. If she's on one of her escapades, she's almost certain to be hiding in Paris. As a child, when she went off, it was always in the direction of Paris. As though she was fascinated by it.'

It was no good. In the end Ravinel no longer knew whether his wife was living or dead. They drank each other's health. They drank Mireille's and her speedy return.

The liqueur burned Ravinel's throat. He passed his hand across his eyes. No. He wasn't dreaming. He was still on this side of the frontier. The clock struck eleven. That was something real. So was all the rest. Those firedogs, for instance, each of which weighed several kilos. Forged steel. Not the stuff that dreams are made of!

'And when you see her give her my love.'

Marthe was showing him out. He was at the front door without being conscious of having left his chair.

'Mine too,' called out Germain.

'Yes.'

He wanted to round on them and scream in their faces:

'She's dead. Dead as a doornail. I ought to know since it was I who killed her.'

Something held him back, however: the thought that Marthe would be only too pleased.

'Good bye, Marthe. Don't come down. I know the way.'

She leaned over the banisters watching him go down. At the last moment she called out:

'Keep us posted, won't you, Fernand?'

Ravinel dived into the first bistro and drank two brandies. The time was getting on. Never mind. With a taxi, he'd make it all right. For the moment, what mattered was to get things straightened out.

'Here I am,' he told himself, 'standing at a bar. I'm in possession of my faculties. I reason coldly. I'm not frightened. I was yesterday, admittedly. I was scared stiff, and my mind was in a turmoil, but that's all over now. Right! Then let's look calmly at the facts…

'Mireille's dead. I'm sure of that, just as I'm sure of being

Ravinel. There isn't a single gap in my memory. I touched the body, and it was just as real as this brandy I'm drinking now…

'On the other hand, she's alive. I can be sure of that too, because I know her handwriting and received a letter in it posted yesterday afternoon. And because Germain saw her this morning. It was impossible to doubt his evidence…

'But a person can't be living and dead at the same time. So she must be half alive and half dead. But does that make any better sense?… Call her a ghost, if you like. There's some logic in that; in fact, as far as I'm concerned, it's an adequate explanation, for I *know* such things are possible. But there's Lucienne to be considered. It'll never go down with her mental processes… In that case, what shall we have to say to each other?'

He had a third glass of brandy, as he still had a chilly feeling inside. On account of Lucienne. If it hadn't been for her…

He paid, went out, and hailed the first taxi. He mustn't fail to meet the train.

'Gare Montparnasse. As fast as you can.'

He lay back on the seat and returned to his thoughts. He'd analyzed the situation, hadn't he? Perhaps not. Already he began to wonder whether he hadn't been raving. Things looked different now. He was in a blind alley, and the more he thought of it the more hopeless it seemed. A hunted man—that's what he'd be. A tired man—that he was already. Yesterday he'd been longing to see Mireille and it had seemed quite possible. Now he dreaded her. He foresaw that she was going to torment him. For how could she forget what he'd done to her? Why shouldn't dead people remember?

There he was again! Back in the same groove. Fortunately he was at his destination. He got out of the taxi and dashed

118

off without waiting for his change, bumping into people right and left. The platforms. An electric train slowly coming to rest. A crowd of people poured out of the cars. Ravinel went up to the ticket collector.

'Is that the Nantes train?'

'Yes.'

A strange impatience took hold of him. He stood on tiptoe near the barrier, craning his neck, and at last he caught sight of her, austerely dressed with a beret on her head. She looked quite calm.

'Lucienne!'

They shook hands. It was wiser.

'You've got a face that would frighten the devil, my poor Fernand.'

He smiled ruefully.

'The thing is: I'm frightened myself.'

EIGHT

They were huddled against the balustrade by the Métro, to avoid being swept along by the crowd.

'I didn't have time to reserve a room for you, but we'll have no difficulty in finding a hotel.'

'A room? But I'm not staying. I've got to catch the six five this evening. No help for it. I'm on duty tonight.'

'No! You're not going to—'

'Not going to what? To abandon you to your fate? That's what you mean, isn't it? You think you're in danger... But we can't discuss things here. Isn't there a café somewhere near where we can sit quietly and have a talk? That's all I've come for, you know—to talk things over. And to make sure you weren't making yourself ill.'

She immediately set about the latter business. Removing her glove, she felt his pulse, quite unconcerned about its being in public. She prodded his cheeks.

'You've certainly lost weight. Your skin's a nasty yellow color and your eyes are dull.'

That was Lucienne's strength: not to bother about other people or what they were thinking, least of all what they might be thinking about her. In the midst of yelling newspaper boys, she was quite capable of counting his pulse, examining his tongue, or feeling the glands of his neck. And Ravinel immediately felt safe. Lucienne—she was difficult to describe. She was the complete opposite of all that was woolly and vague. She was decisive, trenchant, almost aggressive. Her voice was clear. She never wobbled. There were times when he would have loved to have been her. Others when—and for the selfsame qualities—he hated her. At those moments she reminded him of a surgical instrument, hard, bright, and utterly inhuman. Logic—that was her strong suit. Well, she was going to have it tested today, anyhow...

'Let's go down the Rue de Rennes. We're sure to find some little place that's practically deserted.'

As they crossed the Place de Rennes, it was she who held his arm, as though to lead him or hold him up.

'I couldn't make head or tail of your two telephone calls. For one thing, the line was bad. And then you gabbled so. So let's begin at the beginning. When you went back home yesterday morning, the body was gone—is that it?'

'Exactly.'

He watched her narrowly, wondering what sort of a fist she'd make of tackling the problem, she who was always apt to say:

'It's nothing to get rattled about. With a little common sense...'

They were too intent on their subject to heed their surroundings. They hardly saw the long stretch of the Rue de Rennes in front of them; it turned gradually bluer, like a distant valley, as it reached Saint-Germain des Prés. Ravinel's heart was infinitely lighter. It was Lucienne's turn to bear the burden now.

'Couldn't the stream have carried away the body?'

He actually smiled.

'Impossible. There isn't any stream—at least none to speak of. You know that yourself. Even if there had been, the body

122

would have stuck at the dam. Only a torrent could have swept it over that. No. It must have been taken away or I'd have found it at once. You don't imagine I didn't look everywhere before telephoning, do you?'

'I suppose you must have.'

She was frowning now, and in spite of the seriousness of the situation, he couldn't help being delighted at seeing her baffled.

'Someone might have stolen the body in order to blackmail you,' she suggested halfheartedly.

'Once again—impossible.'

He spoke didactically, almost condescendingly, as though to humble her.

'Impossible. I thought so myself at first, but it wouldn't wash. I even went and questioned the postman's daughter, who brings her goat every morning to the field just behind—'

'You did that? You didn't make her suspicious, I hope?'

'I was careful what I said. I didn't give anything away. Besides, she's a bit simple—nobody'd listen to her… In any case, why should anybody want to steal the body? If he knew anything, he could blackmail me without that. No. Blackmail's out. There are other reasons too. Wait till you've heard the rest… But here's a little café—just what we're looking for.'

A couple of spindly trees in tubs flanked the entrance. A tiny bar. Three tables clustered round a stove. The proprietor sat reading the day's sports news.

'No. We don't serve lunches… But if sandwiches would do… Fine… And two glasses of beer.'

He disappeared into a poky little hole in back. Ravinel pulled out a table to allow Lucienne to get round to the other side. Buses stopped outside, their brakes screeching, dropped

123

a passenger or two, and started off again. Lucienne took off her beret and leaned forward with her elbows on the table.

'Now. What's this story of a special delivery?'

She held out her hand for it, but he shook his head.

'It's in the house. I haven't been back for it. But I know it by heart. *I've got to go away for two or three days. It's nothing serious, so don't be alarmed. I'll explain it all later. Meanwhile you'll find plenty to eat in the cellar. Finish up the old pot of jam before—*'

'What? Jam?'

'Jam, yes. That's what she said word for word. *Finish up the old pot of jam before opening a fresh one, and remember to turn off the gas when you've finished with the oven. You so easily forget…*'

Lucienne gave him a keen, piercing look. After a moment's silence she added:

'You recognized the writing, of course.'

'Of course.'

'Writing's easily copied.'

'I know. But there's the style too. It's Mireille all over. I'm positive she wrote it.'

'And the postmark—couldn't that have been faked?'

Ravinel shrugged his shoulders.

'And perhaps the postman isn't a real postman either!'

'In that case there's only one explanation: Mireille wrote the letter before leaving for Nantes.'

'You're forgetting the postmark has a date. She'd have had to get someone else to post it for her.'

The man came back with a plate piled with sandwiches and the two glasses of beer, after which he buried himself in his paper again. Ravinel lowered his voice.

'And what would have been the point in her writing like that before coming to see me? If she'd feared anything she wouldn't have written to me at all but to somebody else. And it wouldn't have been about pots of jam!'

'As a matter of fact she wouldn't have come to Nantes at all... No. It couldn't have been written... before.'

Lucienne started in on a sandwich. Ravinel drank half his beer. The absurdity of their situation was suddenly borne in upon him. He could see that his words were having an effect. She put down her sandwich and pushed away the plate.

'I'm not hungry any more. What you tell me is all so—so unexpected... For if the letter wasn't written before, it certainly couldn't have been after... And she doesn't even refer to—to anything. Like a person who's lost her memory.'

'Exactly. Now you're getting somewhere.'

'What do you mean?'

'Never mind. Go on.'

'The thing is... I really can't see how... Unless...'

They looked hard at each other, then Lucienne turned her head away as she added in a slightly embarrassed voice:

'Unless Mireille has a double...'

That meant that Lucienne acknowledged herself beaten. So they'd drowned Mireille's double, had they?

But Lucienne dismissed the idea at once.

'No. It's quite absurd. A girl might be astonishingly like Mireille, but not to the point of taking you in. Nor me either. And why should a double come and walk into our trap?'

He still had something up his sleeve, but he was in no hurry. He wanted each point to sink in. The buses still drew

125

up at the curb, then dashed off again with their load of swaying passengers standing on the rear platform. Now and again someone came into the café for a quick one at the bar, throwing no more than a glance at this couple who sat motionless with the gravity of chess players.

'I haven't told you all,' said Ravinel at last. 'Mireille went to see her brother this morning.'

A look of stupor and alarm came into Lucienne's eyes. Poor Lucienne! So proud, so competent, never taken aback—she didn't cut much of a figure now.

'She went up to his flat and chatted with him for quite a few minutes.'

'Perhaps that was the double, not the one that came to Nantes… But that doesn't make sense either. Germain couldn't have been taken in any more than we could. It isn't as if it was only the face: she'd have to have the same voice, the same walk, the same gestures. No, we can rule out doubles. They're all very well in fiction, not in real life.'

'There's another possibility,' said Ravinel. 'What about catalepsy? Mireille seemed dead. She was dead to all intents and purposes—temporarily. Then she came to. As right as rain…'

And, as Lucienne stared at him blankly:

'It exists, you know—catalepsy. I'm not inventing it. I've read cases—'

'After forty-eight hours under water?'

She was becoming incensed and he made her a sign not to talk too loudly.

'Look here! If this is a case of catalepsy, I'll give up medicine and become a washerwoman. For it would mean that all I've learned is just so much rubbish.'

She seemed to have been touched on the raw. Her lip quivered.

'We doctors do know something about death and we don't sign death certificates blindly. If that was catalepsy we'd better start digging up our cemeteries. They must be crammed full of bodies that are only waiting for an opportunity to get up and walk home!'

'Hush! No need to get worked up about it.'

They were silent for a while. Lucienne's eyes glowed with anger. She was proud of the medical profession and of her own position in it. She knew her stuff. She expected admiration, and not least from Ravinel. And here he was talking of catalepsy and trying to teach her her business! She looked at him as though waiting for an apology. When she spoke at last it was in her hospital voice.

'There's nothing more to be said about it. Mireille's dead. You can explain the rest as you like.'

'Mireille's dead. And yet she's alive.'

'Come on! I'm serious.'

'So am I. The thing is…'

Should he tell her what was in his mind? He had never disclosed his secret thoughts to her, but she knew him through and through, knew him as no one else did. In a slightly bookish way perhaps, but none the less pretty shrewdly. He took the plunge.

'Mireille's a ghost.'

'What?'

'I said a ghost. She appears when and where she likes, to whom she likes…'

Lucienne's reaction to that was to grasp his wrist again. He reddened.

'I wouldn't say a thing like that to anybody. What I'm telling you is something that's been germinating, so to speak, deep down inside me… I don't think it's impossible.'

'I'll have to give you a really good checkup,' muttered Lucienne. 'I'm beginning to think there's something seriously the matter with you. Didn't you once tell me that your father…'

She broke off as another idea struck her. Her features hardened and she gripped his wrist till it hurt.

'Fernand!… Look me in the eye… You wouldn't play me false, would you?'

She laughed nervously and leaned over towards him across the table. At a distance anyone might have taken her for a lover holding her mouth out to be kissed.

'Don't take me for a fool. It's time you stopped fencing. Mireille's dead: I know she is. And you want me to believe, first that her body's been stolen, then that it got up of its own accord and is now wandering about Paris. And I, because—yes, because I love you—allowed myself to be put on the rack.'

'Gently, Lucienne! Gently!'

'Now I'm beginning to understand. You can tell me any story you like. I wasn't there. All the same there are limits. So, if you don't mind, drop your little game and come clean.'

'I swear I'm telling you the truth.'

'Really? Then we'll say no more about it. Only, please don't take me for a person who can be told black's white or that a dead person is still alive.'

The proprietor was deep in his newspaper, quite unconcerned with his customers. He'd seen too many couples to be interested in this one. But this silent presence behind Ravinel's back made him uneasy and he took out his wallet.

'The bill, please.'

He felt like apologizing for all the sandwiches left untouched. Lucienne was powdering her face, holding up her bag to look in the mirror. She got up first and walked out without looking round to see if he was following. He ran after her.

'Listen, Lucienne. It's the gospel truth. On my oath it is.'

She walked on, looking into the shop windows, ignoring him. He didn't like to raise his voice because of all the people about.

'Listen, Lucienne…'

It was really too stupid, this quarrel, which he had been quite unprepared for. And they had no time to lose. Soon she'd be taking the train again, leaving him to deal with the situation alone. In desperation he seized her arm.

'Lucienne! You know very well I've nothing to gain by—'

'Nothing? What about the insurance money?'

'What are you getting at now?'

'It's quite simple. No body, no compensation. You've only to tell me the body's gone and you haven't been able to claim the money.'

A man looked hard at them. Had he heard Lucienne's last remark? Ravinel was aghast. Really, to bawl out a remark like that in the street! Things were going from bad to worse.

'Lucienne, I implore you… If you only knew what I've been through already. Here, let's sit down over there.'

They had reached Saint-Germain des Prés. There were some seats in the square adjoining the church.

No body, no compensation. Ravinel had never for a moment considered that aspect of the problem. The seat was wet, but he sat down on one end of it. It looked as though everything was over between them, for Lucienne remained standing. With

129

the toe of her shoe she played with some dead leaves. The whistling of traffic policemen, the whirr of the traffic, the muffled sound of the organ in the church, all seemed to come from another world, a world he had already left... If only he had!

'Are you leaving me, Lucienne?'

'Seems to me it's the other way round.'

He spread out a flap of his raincoat over the seat.

'Come on, sit down... Surely we're not going to start quarreling now!'

She did as he said. Some passing women stared at them. No doubt there was something peculiar in their attitude.

'You know very well that on my side this never was a question of money,' he went on in a tired voice. 'Besides—just think for a moment—supposing I did want to play you false, how could I possibly expect to get away with it? You'd only have to come to Enghien and you'd find out the truth in no time.'

She shrugged her shoulders impatiently.

'Very well, let's leave the insurance money out of it. Perhaps you lost your nerve and couldn't go through with it. Perhaps you buried the body instead.'

'That would have been far more dangerous still. For me. Nobody could then think it was an accident, and I should be the first to come under suspicion. And what would have been the point of my inventing the letter and the visit to Germain's?'

The day was fading, the lights going on one by one. It was the time of day he had always dreaded as a small boy, the time when playthings had to be put away. It was rather the same now. He had to put away his dreams. He realized he would never escape. Antibes was done for.

'Surely you can see that, if I did want the insurance money, it was only to… to…'

'My poor Fernand, you're too self-absorbed. Instead of doing something you go chasing will-o'-the-wisps of your imagination. I'm quite ready to accept the fact that the body's disappeared. The thing is: what have you done to find it? Bodies don't wander about all by themselves.'

'Germain tells me Mireille was in the habit of running away.'

'Oh, shut up! What's the good of talking like that?'

No good at all. He had to admit it was a silly remark. All the same there must be some connection, he felt sure, between that quirk of Mireille's and her disappearance now. He repeated in detail what Germain had told him, but Lucienne merely shrugged her shoulders once again.

'All right! She ran away when she was alive. Now she's dead: that makes a difference. Leaving aside that letter and the visit to Germain's…'

Leaving aside! It was one of Lucienne's expressions. Easily said!

'…what matters is to find the body. It must be somewhere.'

'Germain may be an ass, but he's not mad.'

'I don't know about that. And I don't care. I argue from facts. Mireille's dead and her body's gone. Nothing else matters. So the body's got to be found. If you don't want to look for it, it only means that you're no longer interested in our plans. In that case…'

It was clearly implied by her tone that Lucienne would proceed to execute those plans alone. A priest passed, wrapped in a long cloak. The next minute he had disappeared through a little door.

'If only I'd known,' sighed Lucienne, 'I'd have worked things out differently.'

'Very well. I'll have another look.'

She stamped her foot.

'Not like that. Looking half-heartedly won't get us anywhere, Fernand. You don't seem to realize that you're in a tight corner, or very soon will be. It won't be long now before you have to make up your mind to inform the police.'

'The police!' He was quite unnerved at the thought.

'Yes, the police. When people's wives disappear they inform the police.'

'But the letter…'

'Admittedly there's the letter. That gives you a pretext to hang on for a day or two. So does Germain's story about her escapades as a child. But it's only putting it off. Sooner or later you'll have to go through with it.'

'The police!' he repeated under his breath.

'That and nothing else! You can't get out of it. So if you take my advice, Fernand, you'll stop loafing about waiting for something to turn up, and settle down in earnest to finding that body. Pity I don't work in Paris. It wouldn't take me long to get on the track of it.'

She stood up, gathered her coat round her and tucked her bag under her arm with a briskness that indicated clearly that the subject was closed.

'Time I went. I don't want to stand the whole way.'

Ravinel dragged himself to his feet. It was clear now: he could no longer count on Lucienne. Before, when they'd had that breakdown on the road, had not her impulse been to leave him to his fate?… But what could you expect?

They had after all never been more than two associates, two accomplices.

'Of course you'll let me know how you get on.'

'Naturally.'

They had spoken of nothing except Mireille, and, now that that subject was exhausted, they had no more to say to each other. They walked in silence up the Rue de Rennes. They were no longer together, no longer a couple. You only had to look at her to know that, whatever happened, she would land on her feet. If the police made trouble, it was he and he alone who would foot the bill. He knew it. He was used to it. Wasn't it always he who had paid?

'And you must take care of your health.'

'Oh, you know…'

'I mean it. I'm not joking.'

That was true enough. She never joked. When had he ever seen her relaxed, smiling, confident? She was always looking ahead—months and months ahead. She clung to the future as others do to the past. What did she expect from it? He had never asked that question, prevented by a sort of superstitious fear. For he wasn't at all sure of occupying an important place in it.

'I'm rather concerned about what you told me just now,' she went on.

He understood at once what she was referring to, and, lowering his voice, he answered:

'All the same, it would explain everything… If people could come back…'

She took his arm and pressed it against her.

'You thought you got a letter, didn't you? Yes, darling, you thought you did, and I was quite wrong to get angry about it.

133

I understand perfectly now. One ought *always* to look at things with the eyes of a doctor. There are no such things as liars—just ill people. For a moment I thought you were playing a double game, but I can see it clearly now—the whole thing's been too much for you… And with that long drive on top of it all.'

'But what about Germain?'

'Leave Germain out of it. I wouldn't place any credence whatever in his evidence. Nor would you in a calmer moment. You ought to see a psychiatrist. I think I'll send you to Brichet.'

'Suppose I told him everything?'

Lucienne looked up sharply.

'Very well, I'll have a go at you myself as soon as we can manage it. And I assure you you'll see no more ghosts when I'm through with you. Meanwhile I'll give you a prescription.'

She scribbled one then and there, standing under a lamp post. Ravinel wasn't really taken in. In a confused sort of way he felt that they were acting a scene that was altogether unconvincing. Lucienne was trying to reassure him. But no doubt at the back of her mind the resolve was already forming not to come back, never to see him again. He was to be left to face the music alone…

'There you are. Nothing much in it except some sedatives. The best thing you can do is to get a good night's rest. You've been living on your nerves for the last five days and if you go on like that you'll crack up altogether.'

They reached the station. Second by second Lucienne was becoming more and more of a stranger to him. She bought an armful of magazines. So she could read, could she?

'Suppose I came with you…'

'Are you mad, Fernand? You've got a job to do.'

And to crown it all she came out with the astonishing remark:

'After all, Mireille was your wife.'

She seemed to have no sense of guilt whatsoever. He had wanted to get rid of his wife. She had given him technical assistance in return for a half share in the spoils. Her responsibilities went no further. It was his affair and he must see it through. And the remark which flashed into his mind was hardly less astonishing than hers: she was leaving them high and dry. Them. Mireille and him.

He took a platform ticket and followed her to the train.

'You'll go back to Enghien now, I suppose. That's the best thing to do. Tomorrow you'll have a good hunt, once and for all.'

'Once and for all,' he repeated with aching irony.

They passed several nearly empty coaches.

'Get in touch with your firm. Ask them for a holiday. They can't very well refuse. And study the papers. You might learn something from them…'

Said to console him, all that. Just empty words, spoken to fill up the silence, to keep between them one last bridge open, though in a few minutes it would go crashing down into an infinite abyss. But he fell in with the game, making it a point of honor to keep up appearances to the last. He found her a seat in a new compartment which smelled of varnish. And Lucienne remained on the platform as long as possible, only leaving it when the guard made her a signal to get in. She kissed Ravinel with a vigor that took him by surprise.

'Good luck, darling! Keep your chin up. And call me up soon.'

The train moved, slowly, smoothly. Lucienne's face at the window grew smaller, till it was no more than a pale shape.

Other faces passed, looking out of other windows, and each in turn stared at Ravinel. He turned up his collar. He felt ill. The train melted away into a sky that was full of signal lights. Not till it was out of sight did he turn round and walk slowly away.

NINE

Before going to sleep, Ravinel turned Lucienne's words over and over in his mind.

'Bodies don't wander about all by themselves.' The next morning, after the first sluggish moments of regaining consciousness, he was suddenly struck by a detail which had hitherto escaped him. He lay quite still, his features drawn, his brain in a whirl. Yet it was quite a simple little detail. Mireille's identity card was in her bag, which was still there in the house at Enghien. That meant that, if she were found, there would be no means of identifying the body. Supposing the thieves had dumped it somewhere. That was the point—where do they take unidentified bodies?

To the Morgue, of course.

Ravinel washed and dressed perfunctorily, then rang up the Boulevard Magenta to ask for a few days off. No difficulty. Then he looked in the telephone directory for the address of the Morgue. Unable to find it, he remembered that its official name was now the Institut Médico-Légal. And there it was— Place Mazas, that is to say at the end of the Quai de la Rapée, just opposite the Pont d'Austerlitz. Good! He could find out something at any rate.

He hadn't gone back to Enghien, but had spent the night at the Hotel de Bretagne, by the Gare Montparnasse. When he left it, he had some difficulty in finding his bearings.

Paris was once again immersed in a greenish fog, which made everything look as though it were at the bottom of the sea. The Café Dupont was like a liner that had gone down with all its lights burning. He had to walk cautiously, and it took him quite a time to reach it. He drank a cup of coffee standing at the bar beside a railwayman who was explaining to the barman that all the trains were at least an hour late and that the express from Le Mans had been derailed near Versailles.

'And the forecast says it'll last for several days. In London it seems people are crawling about with flashlights.'

Ravinel was seized by a gnawing uneasiness. Why this fog? And why should it have come on this particular day? A day on which it was more than ever necessary to distinguish the living from the dead!... That was absurd, of course. He knew it. But how could he prevent the fog's penetrating him and mounting to his head like opium smoke? It made everything real and unreal by turns.

He paid and ventured out into the street. As he walked, the lights of the café soon faded behind him: the thick sticky void stretched out in front, pierced occasionally by headlights like unseeing eyes, pierced too by the sound of steps, many steps, but no one could tell whose they were.

An empty taxi passed close to the curb and he pounced on it. But where should he tell the driver to take him? To the Morgue? No, he couldn't bring himself to say that. He hesitated, then mumbled some incoherent directions which the man listened to contemptuously.

'Better make up your mind, hadn't you?'

'Quai de la Rapée, then.'

The taxi started off with such a jerk that he was flung back onto the seat. He already regretted his impulse. What was he going to do at the Morgue? What would he say when he got there? Wasn't he simply walking into a trap? For there was a trap somewhere—there must be—a sort of booby trap concealed under the body.

Traps. His mind went off at a tangent to the strange and varied devices made of steel and wire for snaring animals or fish which figured among the articles he traded in, and which it was his business to demonstrate.

'You bait it here with a bit of meat or chicken giblets... You lay it in the water with the end upstream. The fish doesn't even know it's caught...'

Yes, there was a trap somewhere.

The brakes jammed on abruptly. This time Ravinel was flung forward. The driver swore volubly at some invisible pedestrian, then drove on again. Sometimes he wiped the interior of the windshield with the back of his hand, muttering all the time. Ravinel had no idea what part of Paris they were going through. Perhaps the taxi itself was all part of the trap. For Lucienne was quite right: a body doesn't go about all alone. There must be someone else in the picture. Always from Lucienne's point of view of course. The possibility of Mireille's being able to appear and disappear at will was a matter between him and Mireille alone.

Either way there was a threat. It might come from Mireille or from her body. Why not from both at once? That would be worse still, but it was a possibility that couldn't be ignored.

A row of smudgy lights. Ah! That might be the Gare d'Austerlitz. Yes, it certainly was. The taxi turned and dived into a sort of cotton against which the headlights were impotent. The Seine must be close at hand, but there was nothing to be seen out of the window but a stagnant cloud. The taxi stopped and he got out to find himself enveloped in a silence in which he could just hear the engine ticking, a silence like that of a cellar, a silence which seemed to be warning him.

The taxi went off, instantly swallowed up by the fog. Presently Ravinel was conscious of the sound of water dripping from the roof, and trickling along the gutters. He thought of the *lavoir* and his hand instinctively felt for his revolver. It was the only thing hard and substantial in a decomposing, deliquescent universe.

Groping, he came to a parapet. The fog lay so thick round his legs that he instinctively lifted his feet to step over it. Suddenly a building rose up in front of him. Was this the Morgue? He went up some steps. It was.

A large hall. At the far end a stretcher on rubber-tired wheels. On the right an office. He pushed open the door.

Filing cabinets. A green-shaded lamp which threw a circle of light onto the floor. A radiator with a saucepan of water on it to keep the air from getting too dry. Quite unnecessary, as the fog made everything damp in any case. Here it was mixed with tobacco smoke, beneath which was a faint smell of disinfectant.

At a desk sat a man with a silver-badged uniform cap tilted on the back of his head. Another man was pretending to warm himself at the radiator. He wore a shiny, threadbare overcoat, but his shoes were so new that they squeaked every time he moved. Both studied Ravinel as he advanced cautiously.

'What is it?' asked the man at the desk.

What Ravinel didn't like was to feel the other man behind him. And the squeaking of his shoes grated on his nerves.

'It's about my wife. I've been traveling, and, when I got back, she wasn't at home. I'm beginning to be worried about her.'

The two men exchanged glances, and Ravinel had the impression they were trying not to laugh.

'Have you informed the police?... Where do you live?'

'At Enghien. No. I haven't reported it to anybody yet.'

'You should have.'

'I'm sorry.'

'You'll know better next time.'

Disconcerted, Ravinel turned to the other man, who stood with his back to the radiator holding out his hands towards it and who gazed vacantly before him. He was fat with bags under his eyes and a waxen complexion. His double chin almost completely concealed his collar.

'When did you return home?' continued the man at the desk.

'Saturday.'

'Is this the first time your wife's gone off without telling you?'

'Yes... At least since I've known her. It seems she used to run away from home as a child... But that's so long ago that...'

'What are you afraid of? Suicide?'

'I... I really don't know.'

'What's your name?'

It sounded more and more like a cross-examination. Ravinel was tempted to put the chap in his place. It wasn't merely what he said, but the way he calmly inspected Ravinel from head to foot, meanwhile running his tongue over his teeth.

'Ravinel. Fernand Ravinel.'

If the man's attitude was rude, it nevertheless had to be put up with. The important thing was to find out.

'What's your wife like?… To start with, what age?'

'Twenty-nine.'

'Height?'

'Medium. About five foot two.'

'Fair or dark?'

'Fair.'

The man was leaning back with his chair tilted, holding on to the edge of his desk. His nails were bitten to the quick.

'What is she wearing?'

'A blue tailored suit. At least I suppose so.'

That must have been a mistake, for the man glanced at the other as though calling his attention to it.

'You can't say for certain how she's dressed?'

'No. But most likely her blue suit. Though she might well have a fur-trimmed coat over it.'

'You might have checked up on her clothes. Then you'd have known.'

He lifted his cap, scratched his head, then put the cap on again.

'There's the one that was drowned by the Pont de Bercy,' he said. 'I can't think of any other.'

'Ah! So you've found a—'

'The papers were full of it on Saturday. Don't you read the papers?'

Ravinel had the feeling the man behind him was staring at him now.

'Wait a minute.'

142

The man swiveled round on one leg of his chair, got up, and went out through the door. Ravinel didn't dare move. The other man was still studying him—he felt sure of it. Occasionally one of his shoes squeaked faintly.

The wait was horrible. Ravinel pictured rows and rows of bodies all laid out on shelves. The man with the silver cap-badge must be running his eye over them like a butler who has gone down to the cellar for a bottle of Haut-Brion 1939.

At last he came back.

'If you'll come this way.'

They went along a passage and into a room with a tiled floor and white enameled walls which was cut in two by a huge sheet of glass. The slightest sound echoed and re-echoed. From the ceiling came a crude glare of light. Somehow the place reminded Ravinel of a fish market after hours, when it had been cleaned up. He wouldn't have been a bit surprised to see a bit of ice or a strand of seaweed that had been overlooked. Through the glass a porter came into view wheeling a stretcher.

'Come closer. Don't be afraid.'

Ravinel leaned against the sheet of plate glass. The body glided towards him, and he had the impression he was watching Mireille emerging from the bathtub, her hair plastered down, her wet clothes clinging to her limbs. He smothered a sort of gurgle, his hands spread out on the glass which grew misty from his agitated breathing.

'Well?' asked the man in the cap blandly. 'Is that any use to you?'

No. It wasn't Mireille. Not that that made it any less dreadful. If anything, more.

'Recognize her?'

'No.'

The man made a sign and the porter wheeled the thing away. Ravinel wiped the sweat from his face.

'It does give you a bit of a shock. The first time. But since it's not your wife…'

He took Ravinel back to the office and resumed his seat at his desk.

'I'm sorry… That is… Well, you see what I mean… If anything turns up, we'll let you know. What's your address?'

'Gai Logis. Enghien.'

The pen scratched. The other was still standing motionless by the radiator.

'But, you know, you really ought to report it to the police.'

'Thank you.'

'Oh, that's what we're here for.'

And Ravinel found himself outside, his legs weak, his ears humming. The fog was as thick as ever, and he decided to take the Métro. He knew pretty accurately where the entrance to the nearest station was, and, after calculating a moment, set course for it. By this time the traffic had come to a complete standstill, but there were other sounds, some near, some far, and he had the impression of being escorted by invisible presences in a sort of funeral, solemn and secret.

So Mireille wasn't at the Morgue. What would Lucienne say to that? And the insurance people? Ought he to notify them?… He stopped. The fog was almost choking him. And, standing still, he was aware of the sound of squeaking shoes. He coughed: the squeaking stopped. It was impossible to say from just which direction it had come.

He moved on, and the squeaking shoes moved too. It was clear now where the sound came from—just a few paces behind him.

Hadn't he known it was a trap? A pretty cunning one too. They had sized him up perfectly and had counted on his coming to the Morgue… No. That was nonsense. They couldn't possibly have known… And yet…

Ravinel stumbled over the curb. For a second he caught sight of a shadowy figure, but it had instantly disappeared again in the fog. The entrance to the Métro couldn't be far off now. He broke into a run, almost bumping into people whose faces appeared suddenly, as though by some act of creation, and then melted away into nothingness. The squeaking was still audible. Was the man intending to kill him? Would he suddenly see the gleam of a knife, feel an excruciating pain, then nothing?

But why? Ravinel had no enemies. Unless, of course, you should call Mireille one. And he wasn't ready to admit that possibility for a minute. How could Mireille…

The Métro. Suddenly everything became visible. He was surrounded by real people now, all of them covered with tiny droplets—on their coats, their hair, their eyebrows. At the bottom of the steps, he waited for the man. And, sure enough, he came into view: first his shoes, then the shabby overcoat, whose pockets were bulging.

When Ravinel reached the platform, the man was still on his heels. Perhaps he was the chap that had whisked away the body and this was the time he had chosen to come forward and dictate his terms.

Ravinel got in right at the head of the train. The other got in too, but two doors farther down. At Ravinel's elbow a policeman was reading *L'Équipe*. Perhaps he ought to pluck him by the sleeve and say:

'Look here! Someone's following me. I'm in danger.'

The policeman would most likely laugh in his face. If he took it seriously, it might be even worse. He might start asking a lot of questions… Better leave him out of it.

The stations went by with their enormous posters. Should Ravinel try to give his pursuer the slip? No. That demanded altogether too much effort. To begin with he'd have to think hard. Better wait and see. Was life all that wonderful? Was it worth putting up a frantic struggle for?

He got out at the Gare du Nord. There was no need to turn round to make sure: the man was still there all right. The shoes told him that. Funny to wear shoes like that when you're following someone. But perhaps that was the whole idea: the squeaking was to get him down, break his nerve. Certainly the other didn't attempt to avoid being seen.

They reached the booking office practically together, and each in turn asked for a ticket to Enghien, third single. It was five past ten by the station clock. A suburban train was waiting and Ravinel chose an empty coach. That would force the chap's hand. He'd have to come out into the open now. Ravinel took one of the corner seats and threw a newspaper onto the opposite as though to reserve it. The man got in.

'Is that seat taken?'

'I'm keeping it for you,' answered Ravinel firmly.

The man pushed the paper aside, sat down heavily, then leaned forward.

'Désiré Merlin,' he said introducing himself, 'retired detective of the Sûreté.'

'Retired? Then why...'

Ravinel blurted out the words before he'd had time to think.

'Yes,' said Merlin, 'retired, and I must apologize for having followed you.'

He had very pale blue eyes, shrewd ones, which contrasted with his baggy face. He looked quite good-natured now as he sat with his elbows on his fat knees, a watch chain stretching across his waistcoat. He glanced round him, then began:

'It was by the merest chance that I overheard your conversation at the Morgue. What you said made me think I might be useful to you. I've plenty of time on my hands and twenty-five years of experience behind me. I can recall dozens of cases similar to yours. A woman disappears. Her husband thinks she must be dead. And then one fine day... Believe me, Monsieur, it's better to think twice before calling in the police.'

The train started and jogged along slowly through an obliterated landscape whose only features were a few blurred lights. Merlin tapped Ravinel's knee and in a confidential tone went on:

'I'm particularly well placed for carrying out certain researches, and I can do so quietly without having to report to anybody. Of course I should do nothing illegal, but there's no reason to think...'

Quietly? Ravinel thought of the squeaking shoes and smiled inwardly. He was regaining confidence. This ex-detective had a pleasant face. Why shouldn't he be useful? He must know his way about. In all sorts of queer places too, like the Institut Médico-Légal. His pension couldn't amount to very much, and he was probably only too glad to stumble on a man who'd lost his wife. Perhaps he'd be able to find her.

'You're right—you could be useful to me. I'm a traveling salesman. I'm on the road all the week, generally getting home on a Saturday morning. And the day before yesterday, when I got there I found the house empty. I waited two days, and then this morning—'

'Allow me to ask you a few questions,' whispered Merlin after once more glancing round to make sure they couldn't be overheard. 'How long have you been married?'

'Five years. And I can assure you that my wife has always been a most devoted—'

But Merlin held up his hand. 'We'll come to that later. Any children?'

'No.'

'Your parents?'

'They're both dead. In any case I don't see how—'

'Never mind about that. I know the ropes. Your wife's parents?'

'They're both dead too. She's got a married brother in Paris—that's all.'

'I see… A young woman alone a good deal… Any trouble with her health?'

'None whatever. She had typhoid three years ago. Apart from that she's always been in excellent health. Better than mine.'

'At the Morgue you mentioned certain escapades as a child. Have you ever noticed any sign of—'

'Insanity? Not the slightest. Mireille's always had her head screwed on the right way. A bit excitable at times perhaps, a bit irritable, but no more than other people.'

'Has she got any weapon with her?'

'No. Though there was a revolver she could have taken.'

'Did she take much money?'

'None at all. That is, apparently. For she didn't even take her bag.'

'How much is there in it?'

'Just a few thousand-franc notes and some change. We never have much lying about.'

'Was she—I mean is she economical?'

'Yes. Fairly.'

'She might have been putting money by without your knowing it, and have accumulated quite a lot. I remember a case some years ago...'

Ravinel listened politely. He looked through the window, streaked with droplets. The fog was clearing in places. Had he been right to engage this man? He really couldn't tell. From Lucienne's point of view he probably had. But from Mireille's?... There he was again! Another of those preposterous thoughts. And yet... Would Mireille resent having a private detective on her heels?

The latter was wistfully relating his experience. Ravinel with an effort stopped thinking about Mireille or the future. Things must take their course. So long as he didn't have to decide...

He started. Merlin had asked him a question.

'What?'

'I asked if you were quite sure your wife had no papers with her.'

'Quite. If she left her bag behind...'

The train jolted, then slowed down.

'This is Enghien,' said Ravinel.

Merlin stood up and fumbled for his ticket.

'Naturally, the most obvious explanation is that your wife's run away. If she had committed suicide, the body would certainly have been found by this time. After two days…'

That wasn't very helpful. There certainly was a body and it had to be found. Only, Ravinel couldn't very well tell him so.

And the nightmare began all over again. Ravinel would have liked to ask the fat man for his papers. But of course he'd be ready for that. He wouldn't be taken unawares. On the other hand, why shouldn't he be genuine? Wasn't it quite natural for a retired policeman to want to earn a bit to supplement his pension? In any case it was too late. Merlin was on the platform waiting for him. There was no escape.

'The house is only a few minutes' walk,' said Ravinel with a sigh.

They set off through the fog, the shoes squeaking more exasperatingly than ever. Ravinel had to make a supreme effort not to lose his nerve. For this was the trap all right. And he had stepped right into it. This Merlin…

'Are you really a—'

'I beg your pardon?'

'Nothing… Here, this is my street. The house is at the far end.'

'Can't think how you can recognize the place in this fog.'

'I'm so used to it. I'd find my way home with my eyes shut.'

'Perhaps you'll find something in your mailbox,' said Merlin as they reached the gate.

He looked to see, and Ravinel took the opportunity to get indoors first, so as to remove the letter from the table and the knife which was still sticking in the door. Merlin followed.

'A nice little house you've got, I must say,' he commented. 'Just the sort of place I used to dream of having myself.'

He rubbed his hands, then removed his hat, revealing an almost bald head and a red line left by the hatband.

'Will you show me round?'

Ravinel took him into the dining room, after switching off the kitchen light—a matter of habit.

'Ah! Here's her handbag.'

Merlin opened it and emptied it onto the table. The usual things—lipstick, powder, a purse, a handkerchief, a half-consumed packet of High-Life cigarettes.

'No keys?'

Keys? Ravinel hadn't thought of them.

'No,' he said firmly.

And to head the man off further inquiry, he added quickly: 'Shall we go upstairs?'

They went up to the bedroom. The bed still showed a hollow where Ravinel had slept.

'Where does that door lead to?'

'It's just a cupboard.'

Ravinel opened it and showed the dresses hanging inside.

'Nothing's missing except a fur-trimmed coat. But my wife was talking of getting it dyed, and it's quite possible—'

'A blue suit. You said at the Morgue...'

'Yes. That's gone too.'

'Shoes?'

'All the newest pairs are there. As for the old ones, I really couldn't say how many she had.'

'And the other room?'

'My study. Come in. Forgive the mess. Take the armchair

there. And while we're here we might as well have a drop of brandy to warm us up.'

He opened a filing cabinet and took out a bottle that still contained a few tots. But there was only one glass.

'If you'll excuse me a moment, I'll just run down and fetch another.'

On the whole Merlin's presence was reassuring. The house seemed more homey now. He went downstairs, through the dining room, and into the kitchen. There he stopped dead, peering out of the window, at a shadowy figure by the garden gate.

'Merlin!'

It must have been a ghoulish cry, for the detective came rushing down, pale in the face.

'What is it?'

'Look! There! Mireille!'

TEN

There was no one in the street. Ravinel knew already that Merlin was wasting his time giving chase.

Presently he returned, out of breath. He had been the whole length of the street.

'Are you really sure?'

No. Ravinel wasn't sure by any means. He had thought...

What exactly had he thought? He tried hard to recapture the impression, but without success. He needed to sit down in peace and quiet, instead of which here was this man fussing around and firing off questions at him. They muddled him. In any case the house was too small to contain a man like Merlin comfortably.

'Look here, Ravinel...'

He had decided on his own to drop the *Monsieur.*

'...Can you see me?'

He had gone out and was standing outside the gate.

He was obliged to shout to make himself heard. It was ridiculous. Anyone might have thought they were playing hide and seek. 'I said: can you see me?'

'No. I can't see anything.'

'And if I stand here?'

'No.'

Merlin came back into the kitchen.

'I think we must assume that you didn't see anything at all.

After all, you're not quite yourself. And in this fog anything can look like a person—even the gatepost.'

That was true enough, but Ravinel was certain of one thing: whatever it was, *it had moved*. He dropped into a chair. Merlin took his place at the window.

'In any case, if you had seen someone, you couldn't possibly have recognized who it was. Yet you cried out: "Mireille"...'

The detective turned round, jammed his chin down on his chest, and stared at Ravinel suspiciously.

'Look here! You're not leading me a dance, are you?'

'I swear...'

Why did he always have to swear to people? It had been the same with Lucienne yesterday. Why were they all so reluctant to take his word?

'Just think for a moment. If there had really been anyone there, I should have been bound to hear steps. I was at the gate within ten seconds.'

'I'm not sure that you would. You see you were making such a noise yourself.'

'So that's it, is it? It's my fault!'

Merlin's breath came fast. His cheeks quivered. He started to roll a cigarette to regain his composure.

'Besides I stopped at the gate.'

'What of it?'

'Well, if I stopped, I wasn't making a noise, was I? I should have heard steps. Fog doesn't muffle sounds.'

What was the good of this argument? How could he explain to the detective that Mireille could move about without taking any steps at all? Perhaps she was there all the time, perhaps in the kitchen itself, only waiting for the intruder to go before showing herself.

Of course it was his own fault. The idea of calling in a retired detective of the Sûreté to track down a ghost! It was really a fantastic notion. How could he have seriously hoped for a moment that this Merlin...

'There are no two ways of looking at it,' went on the latter. 'You had a hallucination. In your place I'd go and see a doctor and get the whole thing off my chest—my fears, my suspicions, my visions.'

He licked the gummed edge of the cigarette paper, and his eyes wandered slowly round the room as though he was trying to sense the atmosphere of the house.

'It couldn't be much fun for your wife here. Day after day... and then with a husband who—'

He broke off, put his hat on, and slowly buttoned up his overcoat.

'She's left you. That's the long and short of it. And, to be absolutely frank, I can't see that she's altogether to blame.'

Ravinel winced. So that's what people were going to think of him from now on. All because he couldn't say: 'She's dead. I killed her myself.'

Really this was the last straw. He could no longer count on anybody.

'Then we'll leave it at that,' he grunted sulkily. 'How much do I owe you?'

Merlin started.

'I'm sorry. I didn't mean... And, after all, if you're sure you saw somebody...'

Oh no! They weren't going to go through all that again.

'Three thousand? Four?'

Merlin threw his cigarette down on the tiled floor and stamped on it. He suddenly seemed very old, needy, and pitiable.

'Whatever you like,' he muttered sheepishly, looking the other way as his fingers closed on the notes. 'I should have liked to be of use to you, Monsieur Ravinel… In fact, if anything turns up, I shall always be at your disposal. Here's my card.'

Ravinel took him to the gate, and the next minute the man had been swallowed up by the fog. But for quite a long time the squeaking of his shoes was audible. He had been right about one thing: fog certainly didn't blanket sounds.

Going back into the house, Ravinel shut the front door, and the silence came down on him like a pall. He almost groaned, he almost reached out to the banisters for support, for once again he felt sure something had moved. It was all very well treating him as a sick person: he knew he wasn't suffering from delusions. And Germain. What about Germain? Hadn't he seen her?

On the other hand there was Lucienne. She had seen Mireille's dead body. And she was a doctor. Didn't that prove conclusively that Mireille was dead? Well then?

Ravinel pinched himself and looked at his hands. There was no possibility of mistake: a fact is fact. He went back into the kitchen. The clock had stopped and that gave him a sort of bitter satisfaction. It supplied another confirmation—for would a mentally sick man notice a thing like that? Once again he stared out of the window. Perhaps it would happen again.

His eye caught something—a little splash of white in the mailbox. He went out again and approached cautiously as though stalking a butterfly. A letter. And that fool of a Merlin hadn't noticed it.

Ravinel opened the box. No, it wasn't a letter. Just a piece of paper folded in two on which was written:

> *Darling*
> *I'm terribly sorry I can't explain yet, but I'll be back*
> *for certain some time this evening or during the night.*

It was only a scribble in pencil, but there was no doubt about one thing, none whatever: it was in Mireille's handwriting. When had she written it? Where? On her knee? Against a wall?... As though Mireille had a knee! As though a wall could offer resistance to her touch! The paper, however—that was real enough, a sheet that had been hastily torn from a block, so hastily that part had been left behind. There had been a printed heading, but all that had come away was Rue Saint-Benoît. Just the street. No number.

Ravinel spread the sheet out on the kitchen table. Rue Saint-Benoît. His forehead was burning, his thoughts in a turmoil, but he mustn't give way. He must keep tight hold of himself. He would. He was determined to.

The first thing was to have a drink. That would help. There was an unopened bottle of brandy in the cupboard. He looked in vain for the corkscrew. Never mind! Seizing the bottle he brought the neck down sharply on the edge of the sink. Some of the brandy splashed onto the floor, but he didn't bother about that. He filled a glass and drank half in one gulp.

He seemed to swell. A burning sensation, as though molten lava were welling up within him. Rue Saint-Benoît. He'd got it now. It was the address of a hotel. It couldn't be anything else. In that case he must find it. Whether or not it would do any good was a question which could be left to answer itself. For the moment he must find it—that was all that mattered. Of course she couldn't have taken a room there. That didn't alter the fact that she was putting him on the track of it. She was sending him there. Perhaps it was there that she would make the definite sign for him to cross over and join her.

He filled his glass again, spilling more, but he had more important things to think about than that. He felt as though he were advancing towards a kind of religious initiation.

I'm terribly sorry I cant explain yet…

Quite understandable. There were secrets that couldn't be imparted without certain preliminaries. Particularly as she had only been in possession of them herself for a few days. Perhaps she had hardly had time to grasp their significance.

She was coming back that evening, was she? But that didn't mean that he was simply to sit and wait for her. On the contrary. She had taken the trouble to deliver that note; she had given him the name of a street. That wasn't accidental. It couldn't be. It had a meaning, and what it meant was that something was expected of him. They had each to make an effort to reach the other—he mustn't leave it all to her.

Poor Mireille! How well he understood her now. She wasn't angry—not in the least. She was happy in that unknown world where she was waiting for him, and her one wish was that he should share her joy. And there he was, frightened out of his wits! And there was Lucienne who could only think of the body! The body simply didn't count, though the people of this world were so obsessed by it they couldn't see beyond their noses. Lucienne was a materialist whose mind was shut to all that was unseen. Like everyone else for that matter. Like Merlin for instance.

All the same it was odd he shouldn't have found the letter. Wasn't that solid enough? Or was it only visible to certain people?

It was after two. Ravinel went and opened the garage. He'd think about lunch later. Food: that was another thing that didn't really matter. He started up the engine and backed out the car. The fog had changed color. It was now blue-gray, as though darkness were already falling. He shut the garage again, as a matter of habit, then drove off.

A strange journey suspended in the clouds. For there was no solid ground, no road, no houses, nothing but wandering lights, floating like himself in a world of cold, damp smoke. It was hard going, and Ravinel felt heavy and dull. A vague nameless pain gnawed at his guts. At last he reached Saint-Germain des Prés, where he parked the car and made for the Rue Saint-Benoît.

A short street, fortunately. Ravinel started down the left-hand side, and almost immediately came to the first hotel, a small residential one with no more than twenty-five keys hanging up behind the reception desk.

'Can you tell me if there's a Madame Ravinel staying here?'

A cool, critical look. For he was unshaven and carelessly dressed. It wasn't surprising if he didn't inspire much confidence. All the same the register was consulted.

'No. There's no one of that name here.'

'Thank you.'

The second hotel, a little more luxurious but still modest. No one at the desk. He went into a small empty lounge. A few wicker chairs, a plant in a pot, a few dog-eared timetables on a low table. Retreating, he called out: 'Is anyone there?'

His voice echoed strangely. He could hardly believe it was his own. They certainly seemed pretty casual in this hotel. Not only could people walk in and out freely, but anyone could ransack the drawers of the desk if he felt inclined to.

'Is anyone there?'

A sound of dragging feet, in slippers. An old man with watery eyes emerged from behind the scenes. A black cat circled round him, rubbing against his legs, its tail erect and trembling.

'Can you tell me if there's a Madame Ravinel staying here?'

The old man held his hand up to his ear.

'Madame Ravinel.'

'Yes, yes. I heard you.'

He shuffled up to the desk onto which the cat promptly jumped. It sat there staring at Ravinel with half-closed eyes, while the man put on some metal-rimmed glasses and began turning over the pages of the register.

'Ravinel… Yes. The name's here all right.'

The cat's eyes were now reduced to tiny slits. After trying various positions, it coiled its tail round in front over its white-spotted feet. Ravinel undid his raincoat, then his jacket and thrust a finger inside his collar.

'I said: Madame Ravinel.'

'Exactly! I'm not deaf. Madame Ravinel—Here you are.'

'Is she in?'

The man took off his spectacles and with his watery eyes studied the set of pigeonholes for letters, which served also as key board.

'Her key's there. She must be out.'

Which key was he looking at?

'Has she been gone long?'

The old man shrugged his shoulders.

'If you think I've got time to keep an eye on everybody. They come and go, and it's no one's business but theirs.'

'Have you seen Madame Ravinel?'

The man stroked the cat thoughtfully, his eyes wrinkling.

'Let me see now... Still young, isn't she? And fair. With a fur collar on her coat...'

'Has she spoken to you?'

'Not to me. My wife booked her in.'

'But you've heard her speak, I suppose?'

The old man blew his nose and wiped his eyes.

'From the police, are you?'

Ravinel was taken aback.

'No. No. She's... she's just a friend... I've been looking for her for the last few days. Did she have any luggage?'

'No.'

The tone had become curt. But Ravinel risked one more question.

'Have you any idea when she'll be back?'

The old man shut the book with a slam and put his spectacles back into a case that had gone green with age.

'There's no knowing. Least of all with her. When you think she's out she's in. When you think she's in she's out. Afraid I can't tell you anything about her.'

'Just a moment. Can I leave my card for her?'

He pulled one out of his wallet, and the man put it in the pigeonhole of No. 19. Ravinel left and plunged into the first café he came to. His mouth seemed like leather.

He sat down in a corner.

'Cognac.'

Was she really there? From what the man said, he didn't seem any too certain of her existence. When he thought her in one place, she'd be in another. And no luggage, nothing tangible to confirm her reality. It fitted in with the rest. What would that old dodderer say if he knew what sort of a visitor he had taken in? Of course Ravinel ought really to have talked to the man's wife. She was the one who had actually dealt with Mireille. But it was like that all along the line. At first sight the evidence seemed overwhelming, but when you looked closer it turned out to be slightly oblique.

Ravinel paid for his drink and went back to the hotel, which was only a few steps away. Once again there was nobody about. His visiting card was still there, with the key of No. 19 hanging just above it. He crept up on tiptoe, holding his breath. Cautiously he unhooked the key, making sure it didn't click against the attached number plate.

No. 19 would no doubt be on the second floor. The stair carpet was old and worn, but the stairs didn't creak. He had to feel his way up, as there was no light burning. Altogether there was something queer about this dead-and-alive hotel.

The first-floor landing was so dark that Ravinel took the risk and lit his lighter. It showed him a brown-carpeted corridor, which certainly couldn't serve more than eight or ten rooms, so on he went, up to the second floor. Now and again he looked down over the banisters. Right at the bottom, in the basement, was a pale sickly light and in it something which was probably a bicycle… Had Mireille singled out this hotel as the most suitable place to take refuge in? Refuge? You didn't need a refuge—not where she was. It was different with him, and if he could summon up the courage…

The second-floor landing. Holding up his lighter, Ravinel studied the numbers on the doors. 15… 17… 19… He put the lighter out and listened. Somewhere or other some water was gurgling down a waste pipe. Should he go in? Perhaps he'd find a dripping-wet body on the bed… No. He banished the thought, or did his best to by trying to concentrate on some concrete object. He was trembling. And his breathing was no doubt audible in the room.

Striking a light, he found the lock and inserted the key. Then he waited again. Nothing stirred. How absurd it was, this nameless terror! What had he to fear? Were not Mireille and he the best of friends now?

He opened the door and went in.

There was little light in the room, but he could see at a glance there was nobody there. All the same he had to muster all his strength to cross over to the window and draw the curtains. With that done, he switched on the light.

An iron bed, a table with a stained tablecloth, a painted wardrobe, a seedy easy chair. One thing, however, proved that the room had been recently occupied—scent. What's more it was the scent Mireille always used. He couldn't be mistaken. Sometimes it was very faint, at others he got a strong whiff of it. It was only an ordinary Coty perfume, and admittedly there were thousands of women who used it. So perhaps it was only a coincidence. But what about the comb on the glass shelf over the washbasin?

Ravinel picked it up and his pulse quickened. No. There was no room for coincidence here. He had bought it himself at Nantes in a shop in the Rue de la Fosse. Moreover the last tooth was broken halfway up. There couldn't be two combs like that in Paris. Lastly, there were some golden hairs clinging to the teeth.

Then there was still another piece of evidence: a half-smoked High-Life cigarette lying in an ashtray. Mireille never bought any other brand. It was the name that attracted her, for she didn't like them particularly.

Ravinel sat down on the bed. He would have liked to bury his head in the pillow and sob his heart out.

'Mireille,' he kept muttering, 'Mireille…'

If it hadn't been for those hairs it wouldn't have been so painful. For they were golden. The hair that kept haunting his memory was dark with wet and plastered down on her forehead.

Apart from the scent, there were only these two things of Mireille's. She had made him a sign which had brought him to the hotel. Were these signs too? And, if they were, what was she wanting of him?

He stood up. He looked in the wardrobe and in all the drawers. Nothing. He put the comb in his pocket. In the early days of their marriage he had sometimes combed Mireille's hair in the morning, when it would fall onto her naked shoulders. Sometimes he would bury his face in it to inhale its scent of new-mown hay.

Yes. That was the sign. Mireille didn't want to leave that comb at home where it had become something prosaic by contact with everyday things. Here it was different. In this dreary impersonal room it shone brightly in token of the days of their love. It was quite clear now. Quite clear too that she couldn't explain a thing like that. He had to come halfway to meet her before she could come to him.

For she would come. He could no longer doubt it. She had said so in her last note and she would be as good as her word. Come? At all events she would make herself visible to his eyes. The initiation was practically over now. This was to be their nuptial night. Feverish as he was, he was suddenly calm. He put the half-smoked cigarette in his mouth, trying not to think of the lips that had held it before. Striking a light, he inhaled a deep draught of smoke. There! He was ready. He took a last look round this room in which, in spite of himself, he had made a resolution, though it was one he dared not put into words.

He went out and shut the door. Darkness. Except for two phosphorescent points of light at the end of the passage. A little earlier he might have fainted at the sight of them. Now he walked steadily towards the two eyes which, as he came closer, turned out to be the cat's. It came down with him.

Ravinel now made no attempt to silence his steps. On the ground floor the cat gave one heart-rending mew, which promptly brought the old man out from what was doubtless the kitchen.

'She wasn't there, was she?' he asked simply.

'Yes,' answered Ravinel, hanging up the key.

'Just what I told you. You think she's out and she's there all the time. She's your wife, isn't she?'

'Yes. My wife.'

The old man nodded as though he'd known all along. Then, as though talking to himself, he added:

'With womenfolk you need a lot of patience.'

With that observation, he slouched off, followed by his cat. Ravinel was beyond surprise. He realized he had stepped into a world in which the normal laws of existence no longer applied. As he went out into the street, he could feel his heart beating quickly, as though he had drunk several cups of strong coffee. The fog was thicker than ever, and with every breath a damp chill penetrated right to the bottom of his lungs. But funnily enough it wasn't disagreeable. On the contrary, it was friendly, and he felt he would like to dissolve and become merged with it. That was another sign. The fog had started at Nantes on the night they had… It was a sort of protective covering. Though to see it that way you had to understand.

Ravinel found his car. It looked as though he'd have to drive all the way to Enghien in second gear. It was just after five.

As a matter of fact the drive home was rather peaceful, but that was because he had a feeling of deliverance. What he had shaken off, however, was not so much a load as boredom, the boredom that had dogged him throughout life. His job was boring, the people he dealt with were boring, and all this hail-fellow-well-met stuff that had to be gone through was boring to a degree.

He thought of Lucienne, but without the least warmth. She was far away; her features were blurred. She had served her purpose in bringing him in contact with the truth. But if he had never met her he would sooner or later have found it out for himself.

The windshield-wiper flicked rhythmically backwards and forwards. Ravinel was quite confident of not losing his way. His sense of direction seemed infallible. As for collisions, there was little danger of them, as there were practically no vehicles left on the road. Ravinel didn't even keep to the beaten track, but cut through unfrequented byways. He couldn't go wrong: he was omnipotent.

He didn't allow his mind to dwell on what was waiting for him at Enghien, but his heart was full of gentleness and mercy. He accelerated and the engine began knocking. Normally he would have made a mental note to have the trouble seen to. Normally. But nothing was normal any longer, and such petty things as that were bereft of all significance.

Suddenly he was dazzled by the headlights of another car, which almost grazed him as he passed. A sudden wave of fear swept over him, but only for a second. All the same he drove more slowly. An accident at that particular moment would be really too stupid. He must arrive home in one piece and with all his faculties about him.

The last turning he took very cautiously indeed. And there were the first lights of Enghien, shining wanly through the mist. He changed gear. Here was his street. He was conscious of being cold. He slipped out the clutch and let the car glide forward on its own momentum. At the gate he gently put on the brakes. He looked up at the house.

Behind the shutters lights were burning.

ELEVEN

There was no doubt about it: lights were on in the house. Ravinel hesitated. He was tired, very tired. Otherwise he might perhaps have decided at the last moment not to go in. He might even have turned tail and run away screaming. He felt the comb in his pocket and, turning towards the end of the street, peered into the fog. Certainly nobody could see him. If they did it wouldn't matter. They'd merely say: 'Ah, Monsieur Ravinel's back,' and go on to talk of something else.

Getting out of the car, he walked towards the gate. Everything was exactly as it always was. He'd find Mireille in the dining room, sewing. She would look up from her work when she heard his step.

'Well, darling,' she would say, 'you must be worn out after driving through this fog.'

He would take off his shoes before going upstairs to change, so as not to dirty the stair carpet. His slippers would be on the bottom stair ready for him. After that…

Ravinel thrust his key into the lock and opened the front door. He had come home. All the rest was obliterated. He had never killed Mireille. He loved her. He had always loved her. In a moment of aberration he had thought he was sick of the daily round of his jog-trot existence. But that had never been serious. No. Mireille was the one he loved. He would never see Lucienne again.

He went into the hall. The light was on. So was the one over the sink in the kitchen. As he shut the front door behind him, he automatically called out:

'It's me—Fernand.'

He sniffed. A smell of ragout. On the kitchen stove two saucepans were simmering, and the gas under them had been carefully turned down to little blue beads. The tiled floor had been washed, the clock wound up. It was ten past seven. Everything was bright, clean and tidy, and the ragout filled the room with a pleasant, welcoming smell. In spite of himself, Ravinel peeped into one of the saucepans. Mutton with haricot beans, a favorite dish of his. How thoughtful! Too much so. This intimate homeliness, this atmosphere of peace and… and kindness… It was almost too much of a good thing. He would have really preferred to come home to a more dramatic scene.

He leaned against the table. His head swam. He must talk to Lucienne about that, and she'd give him some medicine for it… To Lucienne? In that case… He gasped like a diver coming up to the surface from the depths.

The dining-room door was half open, and the light was on there too. Through the doorway he could see a chair and one corner of the table covered with a fancy blue tablecloth the pattern of which consisted of a series of alternate coaches and turrets. Mireille had chosen it because it reminded her of some old fairy tale. Was Mireille sitting by the fire? For she generally lit a fire there in damp weather.

He stood outside the door, his head lowered, as though under a weight of guilt. It wasn't that he was looking for his words, still less trumping up excuses. It was simply that his body refused to advance another step. And he suddenly realized that there were two Ravinels, just as there were two Mireilles. There were the two spirits seeking each other, and the two bodies repelling each other. The fire had been lit; he could hear it crackling now. Of course. Poor Mireille! She'd need some warming up after lying two days in cold water! No. That was wrong. It had never happened.

It was with a trembling hand that he pushed the door open a little farther. He could now see that the table was laid. His napkin was there in its boxwood ring. The light shone down on the carafe. Everything was in its place and welcoming him.

'Mireille!'

It was as though he were asking permission to enter the room. With a renewed effort he finally flung the door wide open. But there was no one on the sofa in the corner by the fireplace. Behind the brass fireguard, the fire flickered gaily. The table was laid for two. Ravinel was still in his raincoat. He took it off and threw it onto a chair. Ah! On Mireille's plate was a note. This time it was written on their own note-paper.

> *My poor darling*
>   *Everything seems to be going wrong. Have your supper. Don't wait for me. I'll be back later.*

It was hardly necessary to study the handwriting, yet he did so. The puzzling thing was why she hadn't signed the last two notes. Perhaps, where she was now, names didn't count for so much. Nor perhaps did individuality. Such individuality as there was was vague and undefined. It must be marvelous. To get away from that burdensome thing 'self,' with its own particular trajectory which we call fate, and its own particular label of a name! Ravinel to boot! The absurd name given to him by that pedantic little schoolmaster who had made his youth a misery. Yes, it must be wonderful. It offered hope.

He sat down heavily in the easy chair and began to unlace his shoes. When Mireille came back, he'd explain everything to her. Everything. Beginning at the very beginning, that is to say at Brest. For that's where everything had started. They had neither of them ever talked about their childhood. Too shy no doubt. What did he know of Mireille's? She had suddenly sailed into his life at the age of twenty-four. Up to then her life was a closed book, and it had remained so. Ten years earlier she had been a girl of fourteen. Of course. But what did that tell him? Nothing. It didn't tell him whether she was afraid of the dark, for instance, or what sort of games she played. Perhaps she too had played the secret fog game. What had she talked about with her young friends? And why had she had those sudden irresistible urges to run away?

They had lived so close together, yet they had never realized that they suffered from the same nameless ill. They had felt cramped there in that too quiet little house. They had wanted to be elsewhere. Anywhere. Even in Paradise. For he had always believed in Paradise. He had heard about it from Sister Madeleine in the catechism class. She was very old and on the subject of sin was apt to speak violently, even venomously. But when she spoke of Paradise it was impossible not to believe her. She used to describe it as though she'd actually seen it, as a huge park scintillating with light. Full of wild animals too, but gentle ones with large pathetic eyes. And flowers, strange ones, blue and white. Finally she would add, looking down at her work-stained hands:

'And there'll be no more work to do, no more work at all.'

It used to make him feel sad and happy at the same time. But he knew already that Paradise was a place it would be very difficult to get into.

He got up and carried his shoes into the kitchen, putting them down in their proper place, on the shelf by the cupboard. His slippers were waiting for him at the foot of the stairs. He had bought them at Nantes in a shop near the Place Royale. It was silly to think of a thing like that, but in the over-excited state of his mind his memory was sharpened, filling his head with trivial details.

He turned out the gas. He wasn't hungry. Mireille wouldn't be hungry either. She couldn't be. He walked upstairs slowly one hand pressed to his side. All the lights were on, in the bedroom, in the study, and even on the landing. They gave the house a festive air. It had been like that when they first came to take possession of it, and Mireille had clapped her hands for joy.

Upstairs, he mooched about, not knowing what to do with himself. He had a slight headache. The bed had been tidied, and the empty bottle was no longer under the wardrobe. The study too was spick and span. He sat down at his desk, in front of a pile of folders of various colors.

What were they doing there? Oh, yes. His firm had asked him for a report. On what? He couldn't remember. It was all so far away, and so utterly unimportant. A faint sound came from the direction of the street. He went quickly back into the bedroom and stood listening at the window. A man's step. A door shutting. One of the neighbors, the railway man, coming home.

Ravinel was in the study again. He left all the doors open so as not to be caught unaware. The faintest tread or rustle of a skirt would warn him of Mireille's presence. Why did he start going through all his drawers? Was he endeavoring to sum up his life and find a meaning in it? Or was he merely trying to occupy his mind, to fix his attention on something? Downstairs the clock was ticking faintly. It was a little after half past seven.

The drawers were full of papers of all sorts—drafts of reports he had written to the firm, circulars and other publicity material for the lines he traveled in, photographs and newspaper cuttings, mostly about fishing—futile all of them and bearing witness to a futile life.

In the left-hand drawer were the materials from which he made his flies. Here was something different: no one could call this futile. He felt a twinge of regret. In his way he had been an artist. He had invented new flies, as horticulturists invent new flowers. In the firm's catalogue there was a whole page devoted to 'Ravinel flies.' The drawer was divided into compartments containing the partridge feathers, cock's hackles, fur, and tying silk, with which he had made these delicate little creatures. One compartment was full of them, and they lay there huddled like insects struck down in a heap at the foot of a wall by the chill air of evening. It wasn't exactly a pretty sight. They might be artificial, but that didn't make them any the less a picture of massacre.

He shut the drawer again quickly. He had toyed with the idea of writing a monograph on flies. He wouldn't be able to now. That was a loss. It might have been something really worth while.

Come on! None of that! He mustn't soften. He listened. The silence was so complete, so absolute, that it seemed to him that he could hear the trickle of the stream in the lavoir.

It was an illusion, of course. What's more: it was a disagreeable one which had to be banished promptly. He dived into another drawer, in which, beneath a heap of carbon copies of letters, he found some old prescriptions. They dated from the time before his marriage when he had persuaded himself he was suffering from cancer. He had lost all appetite and had been unable to sleep, till one day he realized that he had simply raised a bogey to frighten himself. A sort of self-flagellation. He had become fascinated by the word cancer and took a sort of perverted pleasure in picturing it as a kind of spider devouring his guts. They had had any amount of spiders in the house at Brest, and he had always been at the same time afraid of them and fascinated. They might even have had something to do with his taking up flies later on, but that of course was mere speculation.

A stair creaked and Ravinel pricked up his ears. It was one single creak and nothing more—probably merely the oak in the staircase working. And all at once this brightly lit house seemed to become mournful. If Mireille were suddenly to appear there in the doorway he felt that he would hear the same sort of sound inside him. Something would crack and he would fall to the ground in splinters. That's what he felt, but of course it didn't mean anything. He'd felt the cancer, hadn't he? Yet he was still alive. It took a lot to kill a human being. It had taken two heavy andirons to…

Shut up! No more of that! He got up, pushing back his chair to make a noise and break the spell. For a minute or two he paced up and down the study, then went into the bedroom and opened the wardrobe. The dresses were all there, hanging from the rod at the top, in a pungent atmosphere of mothball.

Why had he opened the door? What had he expected to find there? He slammed it to again and went downstairs.

Silence! It was the silence of the place that...

Generally he could hear the trains going by. Did the fog blanket sounds after all? More likely it stopped them running. It stopped everything. Everything except that exasperating clock. Nine fifteen. She was never as late as this. At least...

He shrugged his shoulders. He was getting in a muddle; he was losing his grip. Something must have happened to Mireille: she had met with an accident. The trouble was that the ideas of *before* got mixed up with those of *afterwards*, and they turned slowly round and round in his cranium, pressing against its bones.

The dining-room fire was dying down. He ought to fetch some more wood from the cellar. But he hadn't the courage. It might well be in the cellar that they had set the trap. Who? What trap? There wasn't one.

He poured himself out a little wine, which he sipped gingerly. How late she was! He went upstairs again, heavily. His whole body was heavy. What if she didn't come? Was he to wait all night for her? And if she didn't come in the morning? How long could he hold out?

Not much longer. Not much. If she didn't come to him, he'd have to take matters in his own hands. He took out his revolver, warm from his pocket with a nice living warmth. Lying in his hand, it was nothing but a bright shining toy. With his thumb he pressed up the safety catch. He had never really understood the mechanism of a revolver. For that matter, he had never understood how a man could press the barrel to his own temple or to his chest. But what was the point of going into that? Obviously that was not what was going to happen to him.

He put it back into his pocket and sat down once more at his desk. Perhaps it wouldn't be a bad idea to write to Lucienne. On second thoughts, no. She wouldn't believe what he said. She'd think he was deliberately lying. What did she really think of him? There was no longer any point in pretending things were otherwise: she thought of him as a second-rater. That was the sort of thing you knew all the time, however much you might pretend the contrary, that you had known right from the start. So she despised him, did she? No, it wasn't exactly that. She just took him for a man who had no inward drive. Which of course was perfectly true. He hadn't. He had gone on too long allowing other people to think for him, decide for him, and make him lead a life that wasn't of his own choosing. Even Mireille: she was one of them too.

But hadn't Lucienne been attracted by him? If not, why had she taken such an intense interest in him, studying his reactions, analyzing his character? And there were moments when her manner was positively tender. She seemed to be encouraging him, holding out a helping hand. At such moments she could speak quite sweetly, too, of their future. She was never very precise about it, but that didn't alter the fact that her words contained more than a hint of promise. Admittedly she had often been sweet and gentle with Mireille too. But that—it was like chatting genially with her patients when they were going to die.

Mechanically, he rummaged among some more papers, bringing some photographs to light. Mireille taken with the Kodak he had given her. That must have been only a few days before she fell ill with typhoid. There was also a snapshot of Lucienne taken about the same time. He compared the two. How graceful she was, Mireille! Slim as a boy and appealing, with those large candid eyes, which were focused on the camera but which saw farther, infinitely farther, right through the camera and right through him, as though he was standing between her and her future, between her and something she had long been waiting for.

In the other, Lucienne was just as she always was, impersonal, almost stern, her shoulders square, her chin a bit heavy. Not that she wasn't good-looking. She was. But hers was a cold and dangerous beauty.

There wasn't a single snapshot of him. It didn't seem to have occurred to Mireille to take one of him. Nor to Lucienne either. The only photograph he could find of himself was an old one that had been taken for an identity card or driving license. What age was he then? Twenty-one, perhaps, or twenty-two. He hadn't begun to get bald. The print was already fading with age, but it was still possible to make out a thin face that was at the same time eager and disappointed.

More photographs. And one after the other he gazed at them dreamily, recalling incidents that no one would ever know. It was getting late. Ten perhaps or half past. The damp from outside seeped slowly into the flimsily built house. He was cold and numb and could no longer control the train of his thoughts. Was he going to fall asleep there in his chair? Was Mireille going after all to creep upon him unawares?

With an effort he opened his eyes and got up, groaning. Yes, he had dozed off for a second. He mustn't let that happen again. Not on any account. Dragging his feet, he went downstairs once more and into the kitchen. It wasn't so late as he'd thought—only ten to ten—but he was desperately tired. It seemed ages since he'd had a good night's rest. His hands were shaking all the time, like an alcoholic's. He was parched and thirsty and felt all shriveled up inside. A cup of coffee was what he needed, but he hadn't the energy to make any.

He put on an overcoat and turned the collar up. With that and his slippers and his unshaven face, he looked a pretty sight. He felt like a person in a dream wandering through a house that had somehow ceased to be his home. They had changed places now, he and Mireille. He was the ghost while she was still in the land of the living. It only needed her to come in and he would be pushed back into the shades.

He lumbered round the table, his movements becoming slower and slower. He had no hat on, but it felt as though his head was encircled by an iron ring. Finally, utterly exhausted, he turned off all the lights on the ground floor and climbed laboriously up to the first floor again. There he turned the lights out too, except the one in the study where he took refuge, shutting the door behind him. He had made up his mind: he couldn't go down again. He couldn't face it. After all, he would still be able to hear.

The minutes passed, how many he had no idea, for he gradually sank into a semistupor, incoherent memories racing through his brain. His eyes were shut, but he wasn't really asleep. With what consciousness was left him he listened, listened to the vast silence around him that sometimes turned into a roar like that of the sea heard in a shell. Like the sea, yes. The silence was like a sea all round him and he was drowning in it. Soon he would go under...

A sound, as though someone had moved. Painfully he dragged himself out of his somnolence with the feeling he was re-entering a frame he had already left. What was it he had heard? It had seemed to come from the garden.

A whistle in the distance. The trains were running again. The fog must be clearing.

This time he heard it quite distinctly. The front door had shut. Next, a click as the hall light was switched on.

He was panting faintly like a dying man, and the air seemed to rend his throat.

The kitchen door was opened. So far there had been no steps, but suddenly they rang out clearly. High heels on the tiled floor, the stride curtailed by a narrow skirt. It was Mireille all right. Another click. That would be the kitchen light. Ravinel screwed up his features as though dazzled by it. Silence. She must be taking off her hat. It was all just as usual, just as *before*… Her steps again. She was going into the dining room.

He groaned. He was suffocating. He made a great effort to rise from his chair.

She was poking the fire now. A clatter of plates: she was clearing the table. Then one after the other her shoes fell to the floor: she was changing into her slippers.

Huddled in his chair, he sat with tears running down his cheeks. She mustn't find him like that, but he was incapable of getting to the door to lock it. He knew he was alive. He knew he was guilty. He knew he was going to die.

They were slippered feet this time that were coming up the stairs. They came closer. He must do something. He must break through this brittle frontier which contains our life. His hands groped feverishly.

The landing light went on and shone under the study door. And she was there just behind it.

No. She couldn't be. It was impossible. She was dead.

Are you really so sure, Fernand Ravinel? On which side of that door is the living, on which side the dead?

Then slowly the handle of the door turned. It was a relief. All his life long he had been waiting for this minute. He was now going to cross over to the other side and become a shadow.

Being a man was too difficult.

He closed his mouth on the barrel of his revolver as though he was literally to drink death. In order to forget.

Suddenly with a jerk he pressed the trigger.

TWELVE

'Have we much farther to go?' she asked. 'We'll be at Antibes in five minutes,' answered the ticket collector. Through the rain-splashed window it was impossible to see anything except the lights that drifted by and now and again the trembling reflection of the lit-up coaches as the express went through a cutting. It was difficult to keep a sense of direction, to know whether the sea was on the right or the left, whether they were heading for Marseille or the Italian frontier.

'Hail,' said one of the passengers as a sudden patter rose above the rumble of the train. 'Yes, that's hail all right. Not exactly the weather to attract tourists to the South.'

Was there some hidden meaning in that remark? Mireille opened her eyes and looked at the man sitting opposite her who had made it. He was looking hard at her. She thrust her hands deeper into her overcoat pockets, but that didn't stop their trembling. Would he notice? Perhaps it didn't matter if he did. Couldn't anybody see that she was feverish?

Yes, she was ill. She had known all along that she'd fall ill. How could she expect to have the strength to see a thing like that right through to the end? And that man... He had been sitting in front of her for ages... Since Lyon. No, since Dijon. Perhaps even all the way from Paris. It was impossible to say. It was impossible to focus her thoughts on anything for long.

But one thing stood out clearly: when you cough and shiver like that, it means you've caught something, if not your death of cold, and if you've caught cold that could only be because you've been *wet*. Wasn't that obvious? Even to the man opposite! And if he got that far why shouldn't he guess the whole story right down to the drive through the night rolled up in a canvas?

All the same there ought to have been some way of preventing her falling ill. It was stupid, that. Still more, it was unjust. Dangerous too, as this was something more than an ordinary common cold that had been neglected.

She coughed again and her back hurt. She remembered a friend of hers who had been an invalid for years just because she'd caught cold leaving a dance. T.B. And everybody said:

'Poor thing! And how dreadful for her husband! A woman who spends all her life in bed!'

The train jolted. The man opposite got up. He winked. At least, that's what it looked like, but it might well be that he'd merely blinked to keep a smut from getting into his eye.

'Antibes,' he murmured.

The train slid alongside the platform. What should she do? Sit there and wait?… A *woman who spends all her life in bed*. The words were becoming an obsession, indeed they already were. She stood up, gripping the rack to keep herself from falling. With a desperate effort, she picked up her suitcase and clambered down onto the platform.

She had to fight against giddiness and an intense desire to sleep. Ah, sleep! If only she could sleep. The man had disappeared. The platform seemed endless. Someone was standing on it motionless, not so much as lifting a hand.

How much farther had she to go to reach her? Ten yards? But ten yards seemed more like a mile.

'Mireille!… But what's the matter? You're ill! And are you crying?'

She was, yes, from weakness. But that no longer mattered. Lucienne was strong. One only had to lean on her, to leave everything to her. She always knew what had to be done and was always capable of doing it. Only, it was difficult to hear what she said, because of the wind.

'Are you listening?' asked Mireille. 'I said: is he following us?'

Everything was becoming confused, but she was clearly conscious of Lucienne's firm hand holding her up, and she heard her say:

'Give me a hand, will you? This lady's ill.'

After which there was nothing but blackness traversed by occasional wisps of consciousness—consciousness of being in a taxi, of going up in an elevator, of the wind that prevented her grasping what Lucienne said. Lucienne couldn't understand that all was lost. She must. She must be made to see that…

'Keep still, Mireille.'

Mireille kept still. But she had to speak. She had to explain to Lucienne something that was of the utmost importance. That man… the one who had sat opposite her… who had…

'Nonsense. Nobody's been following you. Nobody's taken any notice of you at all.'

The wind had died down, or at any rate it was incapable of intruding into this peaceful room lit only by a bedside lamp. Was that a syringe in Lucienne's hand? Mireille didn't want an injection. Hadn't she swallowed enough drugs already?

Lucienne pulled down the bedclothes. The needle went in, but the prick was gone in a second. The bedclothes were pulled up again. The sheets were cool. They made her think of a cold bath, of the one she had been put into fully dressed when Fernand thought her unconscious, and got into a second time when Fernand thought her drowned, dead for two whole days. The details suddenly came back to her. It was as though she were going through it all again, and she kept rigidly still for fear of giving away the fact that she was still alive.

It was Lucienne who'd really done everything. What had Fernand seen? Practically nothing. She had been dragged out of the bathtub and instantly rolled up in the canvas. The awful thing had been that drive. How she had ever stuck the cold?... And cramp too... And then to finish with another ducking in the lavoir, with Lucienne making as much noise as possible in case she spluttered.

When Fernand had gone she ought to have followed Lucienne's instructions straight away, instead of putting off... But she wouldn't do it again: she'd do just what she was told. And with that resolution she was immediately invaded by a sense of well-being and security. And her forehead was not so hot... If only she had always taken Lucienne's advice...

For wasn't she always right? Hadn't she all along foretold exactly how Fernand would react? He *couldn't* lend a hand in the drowning; he *couldn't* look fairly and squarely at the body of the woman he had helped to murder, he *couldn't* unravel the mystery, think as he might. In fact the more he thought the farther he'd get from the solution... Yes, Lucienne had been splendid, and though she had had to go back to Nantes, she had kept her finger on the pulse, ready to intervene in a moment if anything went wrong… And supposing he had found out—they weren't risking anything. Attempted murder: that was still crime enough to keep Fernand's mouth shut.

And now Lucienne was there, bending over the bed. Mireille shut her eyes. She felt good now, now that she could ask her friend's forgiveness for having disobeyed her, for having nearly ruined the whole show by that silly visit to her brother's, for having sometimes doubted… For Lucienne was so hard that it was impossible at moments not to suspect her of acting from self-interest.

'Stop worrying,' murmured Lucienne.

There you are! You see! She could hear everything, even your most secret thoughts. Or had Mireille spoken out loud in her semidelirious condition? She opened her eyes. Lucienne's face was close to hers, but it was difficult to see her features clearly. Mireille made a great effort to pull herself together. For she knew she had forgotten something, something important. She hadn't yet completed her task. Clutching the bedclothes she raised herself up a little.

'Lucienne… I put everything straight at home… in the dining room… in the kitchen… Nobody could possibly suspect that…'

'What about the notes you'd written to him?'

'I found them… in his pockets…'

Of course Lucienne would never realize what that had cost her. To go through Fernand's pockets… with blood everywhere… Poor Fernand…

Lucienne put her hand on her patient's forehead.

'You must go to sleep now. Don't think any more about him. He was a condemned man anyhow. Some day or other, he'd have found that way out. It was the only way for him.'

How sure she was of herself. But Mireille was uneasy. There was still something on her mind, though it was difficult to take hold of. She was falling asleep, but with the last shreds of consciousness she was able to think:

'Since he never suspected anything… Since he never gave another thought to the insurance policy—the one he had taken out on his own life to induce me to take out the one on mine…'

Then sleep came and her breathing deepened. Kind sleep! She was never even to know that she had been on the verge of remorse.

The sun was shining. Life was beginning again after hours and hours of unconsciousness. Mireille turned her head, first to the right, then to the left. She was fearfully tired; she was nevertheless able to smile at the sight of a palm tree in a garden, a tall palm tree with a funny hairy trunk. As it moved in the breeze its leaves waved a fanlike shadow across the curtains. It gave an impression of… Mireille groped for a word… of luxury: that was it. The anxieties of the previous day were banished. She had a lot of money. Or rather they had. Two million francs. The insurance company couldn't raise any objection. The stipulated two years were up, weren't they? Everything was strictly in order. She had only to get well.

A phrase suddenly echoed in her memory. *A woman who spends all her life in bed.* A faint flush came to her cheeks. It certainly was a dreadful fate. But it wasn't going to happen to her. Of course not. Lucienne was looking after her. Lucienne would know how to treat her. She was a doctor and a good one too.

In spite of herself, Mireille's mind went back to the house on the Quai de la Fosse and Fernand filling her glass from a carafe. *A woman who spends all her life in bed...* There was a carafe here too, on the bedside table, a cut glass one that split the light up into delicate colors. She stared into it like a crystal-gazer. She didn't know how to read the future in a crystal, but she nevertheless started when the door opened and hastily looked elsewhere, as though she had been caught doing something wrong.

'Good morning, Mireille. How do you feel?'

Lucienne was dressed in black. She smiled as she walked up to the bed with her man's stride. She felt Mireille's pulse.

'What's the matter with me?'

Lucienne looked at her steadily, as though weighing her chances of pulling through. She said nothing.

'Is it serious?'

A pause. Then:

'It'll be a long business.'

'Tell me what it is.'

'Not now.'

Lucienne took the carafe away to refill it. Mireille raised herself on one elbow and with her large eyes peered through the half-open door. From the sounds, she could follow everything Lucienne did. She could hear the water pouring into the carafe, the note rising rapidly as the level rose to the neck. But did it really take so long to fill a carafe? With a forced laugh which ended in a fit of coughing, she called out:

'All the same! I had to trust you, didn't I? Right up to the last moment you could have tossed up to decide which of us it was to be!'

Having turned off the tap, Lucienne carefully wiped and polished the outside of the carafe. With her teeth set, she muttered under her breath:

'What makes you think I didn't?'

———

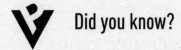 Did you know?

The prolific, multi-award winning duo of Pierre Boileau and Thomas Narcejac wrote dozens of thrillers together, subverting the mechanics of traditional mystery and focusing on unsentimental characters, tension and shocking plot twists. Forsaking the logical investigations typical of pre-war detective fiction, they focused on created disorienting worlds where, as they put it, 'man is out of place'. For a thriller to really hold the reader under its spell, they argued, it must be less about 'who' and 'why' and more about 'how'.

While few English readers know their names, their impact on crime fiction and cinema, in particular, has been considerable. Their novels inspired two of the greatest, and possibly most influential crime films ever made; *Les Diaboliques*, based on *She Who Was No More*, adapted and directed by Henri-Georges Clouzot in 1955, and *Vertigo*, directed by Alfred Hitchcock in 1958.

Clouzot changed several key details for his version of the story—the victim of the murder plot is not the seemingly innocent wife, as in the book, but a tyrannical husband who probably had it coming. Still, the authors praised this liberal adaptation, which they say brought to life in images what they meant to convey in words.

The film version ended with a request to the audience to keep the details of the plot secret, so as not to spoil others' enjoyment of the film, as did the first British edition of the book. We'd like to repeat it here:

This amazing novel is a story of suspense and terror so perfectly constructed that not even a hint of the plot can be given away. The publishers respectfully request early readers to resist the temptation to reveal it.

So, where do you go from here?

If you've not already read it, you really should give Boileau-Narcejac's **Vertigo** a try—another disorienting and heart-stoppingly tense masterpiece.

But if you feel like putting those little grey cells to work on a more traditional murder, Piero Chiara's **The Disappearance of Signora Giulia** could be the book for you—a classic mystery from one of the most celebrated Italian writers of the post-war period.

AVAILABLE AND COMING SOON
FROM PUSHKIN VERTIGO

Augusto De Angelis

The Murdered Banker
The Mystery of the Three Orchids
The Hotel of the Three Roses

Boileau-Narcejac

Vertigo
She Who Was No More

Piero Chiara

The Disappearance of Signora Giulia

Martin Holmén

Clinch

Alexander Lernet-Holenia

I Was Jack Mortimer

Leo Perutz

Master of the Day of Judgment
Little Apple
St Peter's Snow

Soji Shimada

The Tokyo Zodiac Murders
